AMISH WINTER MURDER MYSTERY

ETTIE SMITH AMISH MYSTERIES BOOK 19

SAMANTHA PRICE

CHAPTER 1

FROM THE WARMTH of her house, Ettie pulled aside the curtain and, with the end of her apron, rubbed off the condensation from the glass to clear a circular patch. Now she could see out, and she stared through the softly falling snowflakes at the empty house next door. It sat in stillness, unlived-in, unloved and uncared for. The colorful flowers that had once spilled over the stone borders of the garden had months ago been choked by scraggly weeds. All things in life, Ettie had noticed in her eighty-plus years, came full circle. Just as the weeds had arisen in the fall and smothered the flowers, the winter temperatures were pushing those troublesome weeds to the brink of their own demise.

It saddened Ettie that the house was empty when there were people who needed a home. Any kind of wastefulness was bothersome. The house had been unoccupied since a grizzly murder had taken place there some months ago. She'd known from the moment the Charmers couple had moved in next door that there was something odd about them, and she'd been right. At the time, Ettie's sister, Elsa-May, had said she was being overly suspicious. Elsa-May had been proven wrong and that was satisfying to Ettie in more than a small way.

"Come away from the window, Ettie. You told me you wouldn't do that anymore."

Ettie looked over at her bossy older sister. Being the age she was, Ettie had thought no one would be telling her what to do, but, like other things she'd expected in life, it wasn't reality. "Don't you mind what I'm doing. You just keep on with your knitting. You might slip a stitch if you don't watch out."

Elsa-May chuckled. "I haven't done that in years. I've reached a certain skill level."

Ettie screwed up her nose and took the opportunity to niggle a bit. "Sounds like someone's prideful."

"*Nee* I'm not. I'm just confident that I know what I'm doing. Confidence and pride are two different things." Elsa-May dropped her knitting into her lap. "It's irritating, you looking out at nothing. What is it you see?"

Ettie let go of the curtain she'd held bunched in her hand. "Just snow, and snow, and then some more snow." Snowy, Elsa-May's small fluffy white dog, raised his head off his dog bed. "I'm not talking about you, Snowy. I'm saying there's snow out the window. Go back to sleep."

"He can't understand you, Ettie."

"I think he understands more than you know. He's clever." When Elsa-May stayed silent, Ettie knew her next comment would raise Elsa-May's hackles. "I wonder when we'll get new neighbors." Ettie wasn't disappointed; Elsa-May stared at her, frowning.

"You're scaring them away. Every time that poor

realtor brings people over, they see you staring out the window at them. No one likes to be gawked at and no one wants to live next door to someone like you who's going to be watching everything they do." Elsa-May shook her head and made tsk tsk tsk sounds.

"That's not true, Elsa-May. I only look at them after they've looked through the house and when they're on their way out to their cars."

"And how would you know when they've finished looking if you're not spying?"

Ettie pulled her mouth to one side. She'd been caught out. It was interesting watching what people were doing, and soothing too, in a strange kind of way. She did observe the strangers who came to look through the house next door. What kind of people were they? Why were they thinking of buying the house? Did they know what had happened there? Making assumptions about them had been Ettie's sole entertainment during the silent winter days. "I won't look at all next time. Will that make you happy?"

"Jah. At least it would go a long way to it."

Ettie flopped down onto the couch. It was nearly bedtime and she was bored from staying home for days on end. She had what she'd heard some people call "cabin fever." Nothing ever happened in the wintertime. "It's nearly Christmas again. Another year's coming to an end." She looked up at Elsa-May who continued knitting without saying a word. "How's your arthritis?"

"Not too bad."

"It's cold, isn't it?"

"It usually is this time of year."

Ettie got up and peered into the fire, then picked up the poker and skilfully rearranged the logs.

"Ach, leave it be, Ettie! It's fine. I did that not long ago. I had it just right."

"I know, but I'm making it better."

When the noise of hoofbeats and buggy wheels reverberated through the house, they stared wide-eyed at one another.

"Who's that?" Elsa-May snapped.

Ettie hurried to the window and pulled the curtains aside. The round peephole she'd made moments before had already clouded over. "I don't know. I can't see in the dark. All I can see are the lights of the buggy."

Elsa-May didn't even finish her row before she stuck her knitting needles into the ball of wool and pushed herself to her feet. Since Ettie was already up, she managed to beat Elsa-May to the door.

A black-hooded figure wrapped in a cloak came bustling toward them.

"Helga, is that you?" Elsa-May called out.

Ettie squinted at the black figure wondering what made Elsa-May think it was Helga, one of their friends.

"Jah, it's me," came the voice, to Ettie's surprise.

Elsa-May stepped outside. "What are you doing out this way?"

Helga walked up their two front steps and stood before them. "I just came to deliver some dreadful news."

"What is it?" Ettie asked.

"It's too dreadful. I can hardly say the words."

"Just say it, Helga!" Elsa-May ordered as she dusted flakes of snow from Helga's shoulders.

Ettie was just about to tell Helga to come inside when

Helga spoke. "It's old Ebenezer Fuller, he ... he's been stabbed."

"What? Are you sure?" Ettie asked completely forgetting Helga was standing in the cold.

"Who did you say?" Elsa-May asked.

Ettie grabbed Helga's hand. "Is he ...?"

"He's dead, Ettie," Helga wiped a tear from her eye.

"*Ach*, that's dreadful." Ettie let go of Helga's hand. "Who would've done such a dreadful thing?"

Elsa-May frowned. "Ebenezer?"

"Ebenezer Fuller, Elsa-May," Helga wailed.

"How awful." Elsa-May looked down and shook her head. "I can't believe it."

"No one can." Helga wiped another tear away. "There was a note."

"This is the very last thing I expected to hear." Elsa-May bowed her head and sighed.

Ettie took hold of Helga's arm. "What did you say about a note?"

Helga couldn't get a word out before Elsa-May reprimanded her sister. "Ettie, that's insensitive. The man's been stabbed and you're worried about a silly note."

"I'm sorry." Ettie looked back at Helga. "Have the police been called? Who found him?"

Helga's teeth chattered together. "Can I come inside?"

"Of course." Elsa-May looked at Ettie. "Where are your manners, Ettie?"

"I'm sorry, Helga. Come sit in front of the fire and warm yourself up. Elsa-May will make you a nice mug of hot chocolate."

Elsa-May raised her eyebrows and stepped back inside the house in front of Ettie. Helga bustled past them, took off her hooded cloak and handed it to Elsa-May, who hung it on the peg by the door. Once Helga was seated on the couch, she glanced at Snowy as she rubbed her hands together. "Still got the dog, I see?"

"He's part of the family." Elsa-May sat down in her chair.

"Elsa-May, the hot chocolate," Ettie reminded her.

Elsa-May grunted and then she pushed herself up off the chair. "Well, don't say anything until I get back, Helga. I want to hear about it at the same time as Ettie."

"Denke." Helga said. "I do need some warming up. I don't have a heater in the buggy like some people and it was so cold on the way here."

While Elsa-May headed to the kitchen, Ettie sat down beside Helga. "Tell us everything from the beginning."

"Wait, I said, Ettie," came Elsa-May's booming voice from the kitchen.

"Okay." Ettie looked at Helga trying to keep her questions inside. The woman's skin was paler than normal and she was understandably distraught. Even though Helga was ten or so years younger than Ettie, they'd grown up in the same community. When Helga had married a man from another community, Helga had told him she'd move to his community once they married. When she refused, he'd had no choice but to stay on. That was only a rumor, but that story always popped into Ettie's mind whenever she saw Helga.

Helga put her hand up to her mouth. "It was dreadful, Ettie."

"I know. It would've been." Ettie patted her hand, and then whispered, "Before she comes back, just nod once if you were at Ebenezer's *haus* just now."

6

Helga's brown eyes grew wide and she gave one nod.

"I heard that, Ettie," Elsa-May called out.

Ettie clamped her lips together. Elsa-May's hearing was excellent only when it came to things she wasn't meant to hear. With a flick of her wrist, Ettie whisked the crocheted blanket off the back of the couch and wrapped it around Helga's shoulders. "There. You look nice and warm now."

"Denke. That feels good."

A few minutes later, Elsa-May came out of the kitchen carrying a large tray with two mugs and a plateful of cookies and cake.

Ettie saw there were only two mugs. "You didn't make me one?"

"I could only fit two on the tray, Ettie. You have one of those and I'll fetch the one I left in the kitchen. It would've been faster if you'd helped."

Ettie stroked Helga's blanket-covered shoulder. "I had to look after Helga."

"Denke," Helga said. "You always were kind and thoughtful."

Ettie smiled. "And nothing's changed."

Elsa-May shook her head at her sister before she headed back to the kitchen.

When they each had a mug of hot chocolate in one hand and food in the other, Elsa-May gave Helga permission to tell them what had happened.

Helga's bottom lip trembled. "I hardly know where to start."

"The beginning is always a good place." Ettie bit into a piece of lemon cake that Elsa-May had baked the day before.

"Some time back, and I can't tell you exactly when, the bishop asked Levi and me to keep an eye on him since we live the closest to him."

"And by him, you mean Ebenezer?"

"Who else would she mean, Elsa-May?"

"She could've meant anyone."

Helga continued, unfazed, "I never knocked on his door, but every time I drove past, I'd see him sitting there on his beaten-up old chair on the porch. For two days now, his door has been closed, and there's been no smoke rising from his chimney. I had Levi visit with me to see what was going on. We thought he might be ill. We never expected what we saw when we opened that door."

"*Ach nee.* You saw him lying there?" Elsa-May asked leaning in a little closer.

"*Nee.*" Helga shook her head. "The house was neat as a pin. Fresh flowers sat on the kitchen table as though they were picked today. Who would've thought a man living by himself would bother making the place nice with a vase of flowers? They had to be store-bought too. He had none in his garden."

"Then what happened?" Ettie asked.

"We called out but there was no sound. That's when I sent Levi to the barn."

When she hesitated, Ettie asked, "And that's where you found him?"

"*Nee.*" Helga shivered.

"Stop interrupting, Ettie. Go on, Helga."

"He wasn't in the barn either. When we came back inside wondering what to do, that's when we saw the note. It seemed someone had said they wanted to meet with him. Since he hadn't taken his buggy, we knew he'd set off on foot—if he was meeting the person who wrote that note. We both walked in different directions to find him. We thought he might've fallen and not been able to get back up. Then I heard Levi holler that he'd found him. He was dead. Levi found him not far from the house, in the trees behind the barn. Jack, the man living in between us found him just at the same time that Levi came upon him. Jack picked up the knife and then Levi grabbed it from him."

"Did the neighbor kill him?"

"*Nee.* He said his dog found him. His dog was there with him. He said his dog wanted to walk over by the fence and then his dog ran away. He ran after the dog, and that's when he found Ebenezer at the same time as Levi found him."

Ettie and Elsa-May looked at each other. "And you called the police?" asked Ettie.

"We did. Ebenezer had no phone in his barn, so the neighbor called them from his house. A detective came. He didn't have much to say and asked if I knew you, Ettie."

"Oh?"

Elsa-May finished her mouthful. "That'd be Detective Kelly."

"That was the name, *jah.* He said he'd stop by here. Does he think you killed Ebenezer, Ettie?"

"*Nee.*"

"Of course not, Helga. From time to time Detective Kelly comes to Ettie for help when a crime involves someone from our community."

"I could've helped him. Why would he need to involve Ettie?"

"Why would someone have killed him?" Ettie tapped on her chin.

Helga told Ettie, "The detective thinks it had something to do with the note."

Ettie stared at her. "Is that what he said?"

"What did the note say?" Elsa-May asked.

"Not much."

"Well, what?" Ettie asked.

"I don't remember exactly, but it was something about someone meeting him somewhere."

"Do you have any idea who would've killed him?" Ettie asked Helga.

"I don't know."

"Did he have enemies?" Elsa-May slurped on her hot chocolate.

"He hardly ever talked to anyone, so he can't have upset anybody. There were never any visitors and we must pass by there at least twice every single day."

"Have you told his *kinner?*" Elsa-May asked.

Ettie stared at her sister. "Your memory can't be failing you that badly. The man never married. He was known for his bad temper and I don't think any woman wanted to risk a lifetime with him."

Elsa-May looked over at Helga. "So, he has no one?"

Helga sneezed. Then she took a mouthful of hot chocolate. "How about we talk about this tomorrow? You can come to me. I have to get home to Levi. He's shaken about this."

"We'll do that. We have to get a few things from town. We'll stop by on the way home."

"It was such an awful shock for Levi. I've left him alone while I came to tell you two about the policemen looking for Ettie. I was worried since one of the policemen mentioned your name."

"I think I'll be okay. *Denke* for coming to tell us."

"It was a detective, Helga," Elsa-May corrected her.

Helga shrugged her shoulders. "Same thing."

"Not really."

Ettie patted Helga on her shoulder. "You get home and keep yourself warm."

"I will."

"Take the blanket with you for the buggy."

"Nee denke. I have one in there to put over my knees."

The elderly sisters walked Helga to the door. While Elsa-May opened the door, Ettie helped Helga back into her cloak.

When Helga navigated her way toward the porch steps, Ettie called after her. "Mind the stairs. They can be slippery."

When Helga got to the gate, she turned around and waved. The two sisters stayed put and watched Helga get into her buggy and drive away. When the buggy was a speck in the distance, they closed the door.

"Now all the cold air's in the *haus,*" Elsa-May grumbled. "We're heating the outdoors."

"It'll warm up in here soon."

Once they were seated again, Elsa-May picked up her knitting. "What do you think of that? Old Ebenezer's been murdered."

"Stabbed too, so it's not even a question of it being an accident. If he'd been shot it could've been an accident. That would've been better."

"Ettie! What are you wishing upon the poor man?"

"I'm not. I'm only thinking that if the murderer

11

wanted to get away with it he'd have a better chance if he made it look like an accident."

"Maybe it wasn't planned. It could've been a spur of the moment killing. Ebenezer might've made someone angry with him and then they grabbed a knife and then—"

"We can think up things all we like, but the number one thing we need to do is get a look at that note."

Elsa-May sighed. "Do you really want to be bothered with all this, Ettie? Why not let the police handle it? After all, how well did we know Ebenezer? We didn't know him, did we?"

Ettie stared at her sister not knowing how to answer. Of course she wasn't pleased about Ebenezer being killed, but if she could be some small use to Detective Kelly it did give her something to do. Without a family to cook and to care for, after her chores were done the only other thing to do was sit around the house all day watching her sister knit. Although Ettie liked needlework, she wasn't consumed with her pastime the way Elsa-May was. "You know I can't not do nothing."

Elsa-May's eyebrows drew together. "What you said makes no sense at all."

"Doesn't it?"

"*Nee,* well I suppose it might, but it'll take me too long to figure out what you mean with all those double negatives. Did you mean you can't do nothing—anything?"

"That's right. I can't do nothing." Ettie rubbed her chin. "I'm thinking about the note. Was it from the killer? And, if it was, why didn't he take it with him after he killed Ebenezer?"

"I can't answer that. Depends what it said."

"I know. Instead of just waiting for Kelly to come here

tomorrow, we should set off to Helga's early, and then stop by the station after we see her."

Elsa-May began a new row of knitting. "Whatever you think is best. I do have one question, though."

Ettie looked up at Elsa-May. "What's that?"

"Who's Ebenezer Fuller?"

CHAPTER 2

AFTER ELSA-MAY and Ettie had breakfast the next morning, Ettie stood at the door pulling on her coat. The night before Elsa-May had confessed she didn't remember Ebenezer at all, but Ettie had refreshed her mind by telling the story about Ebenezer being mean to some children by refusing to allow them to take a shortcut through his land to get to their friends' place. From that, Ebenezer got a reputation for being unpleasant at times.

"Are you ready?" Ettie asked, trying to be patient while waiting by the door.

"In a minute, I'll finish the row."

"You know, one thing I can't figure out is even though Ebenezer never married, he'd grown a long gray beard. I've never thought too much about the beard situation, but now I know for certain he wasn't a widower it's definitely odd."

"Hmm," was all that Elsa-May said appearing totally uninterested.

SAMANTHA PRICE

It was usual for the unmarried men in the community to remain clean-shaven and only the married men had beards.

"You've started another row!"

Elsa-May looked up at Ettie. "I'll do some more knitting while you clean the kitchen. You know I can't go anywhere without it being spotless."

"I've already cleaned it. Let's go."

Elsa-May rolled her eyes with the clickety-clack of her knitting needles not missing a beat. "There's clean and then there's clean."

"What do you mean?"

"There's the way I clean and the way you do it."

Elsa-May was always running after Ettie, cleaning where she'd already cleaned. It was an annoyance, and one of her sister's traits Ettie had done her best to overlook. It was easier to go along with Elsa-May's quirks especially when she was anxious to get out of the house. "And will the 'way you do it' take long? We're supposed to be getting an early start."

"It'll be quick if the kitchen is as clean as you say."

"I'll watch what you do and I'll challenge you to find one crumb anywhere in the entire kitchen."

Elsa-May grinned, put the knitting back in her bag, and then pushed herself to her feet. When they walked through the door of the kitchen, Elsa-May immediately put her hands on her hips.

"What's the matter?"

"You've left your cup on the sink." She flung her arm out into the air and pointed at Ettie's rosebud covered teacup.

16

"I'll use it later. I've rinsed it. There's no point putting it away if I'm going to use it again."

Elsa-May didn't say anything. Instead, she marched forward and grabbed the cup. When she held it in her hand and opened her mouth to speak, the cup slipped from her fingers. She went to grab it in mid-air and was unsuccessful and it crashed to the floor. It lay there in several pieces.

Ettie stood there in shock looking at the scattered pieces of her special cup, the delicate white china with the pretty pink rosebuds. It had been given to her by Elsa-May as a gift.

Elsa-May put both hands to her face. "Oh, Ettie, I'm sorry. I'm so sorry."

With a shrug of her shoulders, Ettie said, "It was only a cup. Don't upset yourself over it."

"I know it was special. I'll find you another exactly the same."

"There's no need. I enjoyed it while I had it."

"I'll go back to where I bought it and get you another."

"*Nee.* Don't."

"I will." Elsa-May swooped down to collect the pieces and then cut her hand on a jagged chip. "Ouch! I cut myself."

"Is it bleeding?"

"*Jah.*"

Ettie grabbed Elsa-May's hand for a closer look. "It's not too deep, that's good. Just wash it under the tap and then hold your handkerchief tight against it. You've got one on you, *jah?*"

Elsa-May nodded and pulled her white handkerchief out of her sleeve. "I always carry one."

While Elsa-May washed her hand at the kitchen sink, Ettie collected the broken pieces. Tea always tasted better out of a fine china cup. Now she'd have to drink out of their thicker cups and that would never be the same.

Once the kitchen was clean, by Elsa-May's standards, they made their way down the road to the shanty and called for a taxi.

"Remind me again why we're going to Helga's?" Elsa-May asked when they climbed into the taxi.

"She asked us to come over and talk about things. We can ask her questions. She was too shaken last night to think straight."

"Okay."

"Why didn't you remember that?"

"I did."

Elsa-May looked out one window of the car, and Ettie looked out the other.

When they were nearly at Helga's, they passed by Ebenezer's house. People in white suits were getting into two white vans.

"What's going on there?" the taxi driver commented, craning his neck and slowing the car to a snail's pace.

"Not sure." Elsa-May wound down the window.

"That must've been where the man was murdered. It was on the news this morning."

"What was said?" Ettie asked the driver.

"Just that a man, an elderly Amish man was found stabbed. Did you know him?"

Ettie and Elsa-May looked at one another. "Not very well," Elsa-May answered.

They didn't say another word until they got out of the taxi at Helga's place.

. . .

WHEN THEY KNOCKED on Helga and Levi's door, no one answered. They were just about to head around the back of the house when Ettie saw a note poking out from under the doormat. She stretched down and picked it up.

Elsa-May peeped over her shoulder. "What does it say?"

"Sorry if I'm out when you get here. I'll be back later. I had to go into town." Ettie shook her head and looked at the taxi disappearing over the hill. "Botheration. We'll have to call another taxi. Or, we could walk over to Ebenezer's *haus* and see what we can learn?"

"It's a distance, Ettie, and it's cold." Elsa-May pulled her coat tighter around herself.

"Jah, but would you walk it if it was closer?"

Elsa-May frowned. "I suppose I would, but it's not. I would walk if it was half the distance."

"Let's just do it. We'll take a shortcut through the fields."

Elsa-May looked down at her feet. "Just as well I wore my old boots." Then she looked up into the sky. "What if it snows and we freeze to death?"

"They'll find us when we thaw out." Ettie chuckled. "We'll be okay. We've got warm coats. The walk will warm us up."

"Or kill us." Elsa-May grimaced

"It's only half a mile away."

Elsa-May pulled the collar of her coat up around her neck closing the gap between her coat and her black over-bonnet. "It was silly of Helga to tell us to come and not be home when we arrive. Inconsiderate!"

"She might've had somewhere important to be."

"But still. It was careless, but I suppose we didn't give her an exact time we'd be here. Perhaps the blame lays with us?"

CHAPTER 3

ETTIE LINKED arms with Elsa-May as they trudged through the grass. It could've been a pleasant walk if it hadn't been so cold. It didn't help that Elsa-May kept grumbling about there not being a fire burning to warm them at Ebenezer's house when they got there. And, the fact that the nearest phone they'd be able to use would be back in Helga's barn.

"At least the police and evidence technicians have gone and, by the looks of it, they're not coming back," Ettie said, trying to cheer her sister up.

"Well, we wouldn't have come here if they weren't gone."

Ettie looked up at the house. "Not too far now."

"My legs are aching."

"It's all in your mind."

"*Nee,* it's all in my legs." Elsa-May stopped and rubbed the back of her thighs. "Wait for a minute."

"I'm waiting." Ettie looked up and saw a car stop outside Ebenezer's house. Then a man got out with something in his hand. When she looked closer, she saw it was a camera. "That'll be someone from the newspaper. Let's stay back until he leaves." They moved behind a tree and peeped out, while the man walked around taking shots of the house. After snapping away for no longer than one minute, he got in his car and drove away. "He's gone."

"I can see that for myself."

"Come along. One hundred more strides and we'll be there." Ettie did her best to ignore the chilly wind that was biting into her cheeks and was glad that Elsa-May started walking again.

Finally, they arrived at Ebenezer's house, but they weren't happy to see crime scene tape still around it. "This wasn't here before." Elsa-May ran a finger along the tape.

"Maybe it was and we just couldn't see it when we drove past. That's why that photographer didn't stay long."

"What do we do now?" Elsa-May asked.

"Maybe they've simply forgotten to take it down. They should've gotten all their evidence by now. Otherwise, they'd still be here gathering clues."

"So, what are you saying?"

Ettie didn't say anything, she merely raised the crime scene tape and slid under it. When she was on the other side, she lifted it for Elsa-May.

"*Nee*, we can't. What if we destroy evidence?"

"They've already been here. You saw them leave. They're not coming back."

"You really think they've forgotten to take it down?"

Ettie nodded. "I'll guarantee it."

Elsa-May slid under the tape and they walked up the two rickety wooden steps.

Ettie advised, "Careful where you put your feet."

Elsa-May looked down. "It looks like this porch will fall down at any minute. I'm sure the boards are all uneven too, and look! It's tilting down there in the corner."

"Let's just get inside before we fall through." Ettie put her hand on the rounded metal door handle, turned it all the way and the door opened. "It's open!"

"Good for us." Elsa-May gave Ettie a little shove, to push her through the doorway first, and then wasted no time getting through herself. "What are we looking for exactly?"

"I don't know. Some kind of a clue. It is neat as a pin just like Helga said." Ettie opened a cupboard door in the living room and saw a stack of yellowed newspapers. "He saved all the Amish papers. For years, it seems."

"I'm looking in the kitchen," Elsa-May called out from the other room.

"What do you see?"

"Nothing. It would help, though, if I knew what I was looking for."

Ettie headed to one of the bedrooms feeling a little bad that she was in Ebenezer's house when they'd never bothered to visit him, and worse, they'd forgotten about him altogether. "Do you hear that, Elsa-May?"

"What?"

"It sounded like a car." Out the window, she saw a newish white car and a woman walking to the house. "Someone's coming."

Elsa-May hurried out of the kitchen. "What'll we do? We'll be in trouble if anyone finds us here."

The sisters watched the woman making her way closer

to the house. She had no qualms about slipping under the crime scene tape in between herself and the house.

"I'll have to answer the door." Ettie opened the door just as the woman had her hand on the handle. She looked up at Ettie in fright. "Hello," said Ettie with a smile. The woman looked odd, and she had a large black bag slung over one shoulder.

"Oh! I didn't expect anyone to be here. I heard about Ebenezer." She looked past Ettie at Elsa-May. "Are you relatives of his?"

"No. We're friends. Would you like to come in?"

"Thank you." No one mentioned the fact that they had all gone through the crime scene tape. The sisters stepped aside to allow the woman through.

"How did you know Ebenezer?" Ettie asked, as she eyed the woman carefully. She was definitely odd looking. Maybe it was the pale skin made to seem even paler by her dark hair and the heavy-handed use of black eye makeup. The blood red lips didn't help matters either.

"I was his nurse. I came every few weeks to check on him. I heard what happened and I just couldn't believe it. It's too horrible to be true."

"It's dreadful. Just dreadful."

"How did you hear about him?"

"It was on the radio this morning. On the news. Do they know who did it?"

Elsa-May shook her head. "We don't know."

"We don't know anything at all." Ettie was just about to ask the nurse why she was there, when the nurse put a glove-clad hand to her forehead. "Would you mind if I have a glass of water?"

"Are you okay?" Elsa-May asked.

"I'll be fine. It's just the tragedy of it all with the way he went."

"Follow me."

In single file, the three of them moved to the kitchen. Ettie noticed the woman looking around as she went. While Ettie stood silently, wondering what to say, Elsa-May filled a cup with water.

When Elsa-May passed her the cup, Ettie asked, "Did Ebenezer have some kind of ongoing medical condition?"

When the nurse took the water in both hands, Ettie saw that both hands were trembling slightly. "Thank you. No, he didn't. I only came for his regular checks. He was well." She took a couple of slow sips. "How well did you both know him?"

Ettie tried to be as evasive as possible. "We were in his community and we're all quite close."

"And, for whom do you work?" Elsa-May asked.

"Just one of the local medical practices. Dr. Moore developed a program for the elderly. For those in outlying areas and with no means of transport, or who live on their own with little outside help. Ebenezer ticked those three boxes." The nurse eyed them carefully. "And how are the both of you getting along health-wise?"

"We drove here."

"Elsa-May doesn't hear too well sometimes. We're in tip-top shape," Ettie said.

"That's good and let's hope you both stay that way."

"What did she ask?" Elsa-May said to Ettie.

"She asked how our health is, not how we got here."

"Oh, I'm sorry."

"You don't have to be sorry," the nurse said.

"I am sorry. I'm sorry that we lost touch with Ebenezer a little over the last couple of years," Elsa-May confessed.

"Don't feel bad. It so often happens."

Ettie eyed the nurse carefully. "Might I ask which way you're headed?"

She blinked her thick mascara-coated lashes. "What do you mean?"

"When you leave here."

She placed the cup down onto the kitchen table. "I'm going back to the clinic."

Elsa-May asked, "Near town?"

"Yes. Behind the library."

"Might we be able to catch a ride with you?" Ettie asked.

"Certainly. That's not a problem. I'm happy to drive you. We can talk about Ebenezer on the way there."

"We walked from our friend's place. She doesn't live too far."

Ettie stared at Elsa-May wondering if she'd heard something different.

"We don't even know your name," Elsa-May said to the nurse.

The woman smiled. "I'm sorry. I'm Patricia Stuart."

"This is Ettie Smith and I'm Elsa-May Lutz. We're sisters."

"Nice to meet you both."

"And you as well."

"Do you know when his funeral will be?" She looked from one sister to the other.

They hadn't even thought about a funeral. Is that why the woman had come, to find someone who knew

Ebenezer to offer her condolences? "No. We don't. We've only just learned about his death ourselves."

Ettie and Elsa-May walked into the living room and turned around thinking that Patricia would follow.

A moment later Patricia walked out. "I'm ready to go now if you are."

"Yes, we're ready."

When they reached Patricia's car, Ettie made sure she got in the backseat and Elsa-May sat in the front where there was more leg room.

When they were nearly into town, Ettie cleared her throat, ready to ask a difficult question. "Patricia, why did you go to Ebenezer's house just now?"

She glanced at Ettie in the review mirror. "I was just so shocked and upset. I suppose it was my way of saying goodbye."

"We were all shocked," Elsa-May said. "It was the last thing we expected to hear when our friend stopped by and told us last night."

CHAPTER 4

WHEN SHE PULLED into the parking lot of the clinic, the nurse asked, "Is there anywhere you'd like me to take you? I'm not due to start for several minutes, and it's no trouble to take you somewhere else."

"That's okay. We're going to the police station."

She stared and was quiet for a moment. "The police station?"

"Yes. We're talking to the detective."

"About Ebenezer?"

"That's right."

Patricia unbuckled her seat belt and the sisters did the same. "I might see you at the funeral."

"We'll be there," Ettie said as she opened the car door.

They parted ways and Elsa-May and Ettie walked toward the station. Ettie leaned in close to Elsa-May. "That was odd. Why was she at Ebenezer's house? She didn't even say what she was doing there. And she didn't ask why we were there. She went right through that tape as though it wasn't even there. And, she said nothing about Ebenezer while we were in the car, after saying we'd talk about him during the ride." Ettie shook her head wondering if the nurse was the killer and had come back hoping to remove evidence left behind.

"You thought nothing about the crime tape either."

"I gave it careful consideration."

"Maybe she came there because she was upset and it was her way of seeing what she could do to help. That's what she said, more or less."

"Help who exactly? Not Ebenezer. It's too late for anyone to help him."

"Don't you remember what she said when I asked her just now?"

"I mean the real reason. That was something she made up. There's something funny about her."

"I know. She looked a bit terrifying to me, but we know she's a real nurse at least. She wasn't lying about that." Ettie turned around and looked back at the red brick building full of doctors' offices.

THEY SAT in the waiting area of the police station, waiting for Detective Kelly. When he finally appeared, he didn't look happy. That wasn't at all unusual for him.

"There you are. I went to see you today but you weren't home."

"That's why we're here. Helga said you were coming to see us."

"So, we thought we'd save you the bother."

He opened his mouth like he was going to say something, and then apparently thought better of it. "Let's talk in my office."

Ettie stood and with a hand under her sister's arm she helped Elsa-May to her feet. They followed Kelly down the hallway. Before they got to the doorway, Ettie whispered to Elsa-May, "We can't tell him about the nurse because he'll find out we've been in Ebenezer's *haus*."

He sat behind his desk while they sat in the two chairs opposite. Without saying a word, he stared at them for a moment. "What do you know about Ebenezer Fuller?"

With a deep breath, Ettie said, "We weren't close."

He looked at Elsa-May and she shook her head. "We weren't," she added.

"I don't suppose you knew anyone who wished him harm?"

"No."

"We passed his house to get to Helga's just now. Why was there tape all around it?"

Ettie added, "We thought you would've finished all your evidence searching since he was found yesterday."

Kelly narrowed his eyes causing deep lines to furrow out toward his ears. "I've got some men going back today to do a further search around the house to see if we can turn up anything."

"Outside?" Elsa-May asked.

He gave a sharp nod, then he opened one of the many folders on his desk, and pulled out a piece of paper pushing it across the desk to them. "The coroner tells me the perpetrator would most likely have cuts on his hands. It has to do with the shape of the bloody knife we found— the shape of it, the angle of the stab wounds and the fact that they hit bone. Their hand would've jolted from the impact and slid from the handle into the—"

"No need to go on," Elsa-May said.

Kelly smirked when he saw Elsa-May's reaction. Then he pulled a piece of paper out of another folder on his desk and slid it across to them. "What do you make of it? It's a copy of a letter we found on Ebenezer's kitchen table."

Elsa-May looked over Ettie's shoulder. "Is that all? No date? It could've been to or from anyone."

Ettie ignored her sister, and read out the note. *"Ebenezer, I know you won't allow me on the land. Meet me at the boundary and we'll see if we can work this out."* Ettie looked up at Kelly. "I can't make out the signature."

"It's little more than a squiggle. And to answer your concern, Mrs. Lutz, since your friend told us Ebenezer was a recluse, where would he have gotten the note from if someone didn't go there and leave it at his house? There was no envelope anywhere to be seen, so we know he didn't get it in the mail. We've gone right through his trash."

Ettie wanted to tell him about the strange nurse, but couldn't do so without revealing they too had been inside the house.

Kelly continued, "Boundaries made me think of boundary fences and we talked to his neighbor to the right of him already. No one lives on the other side. It's owned by a mining company and has been for years."

"Who's his neighbor? He's the one who found him along with Levi?" Ettie visualized the farmhouse they'd passed earlier that sat between Helga's and Ebenezer's places.

"That's right. They seem a pleasant couple. Jack Simpson and his wife, Blythe. They've lived there for over ten years and only talked to Ebenezer once when part of the fence between their two properties was destroyed by fallen trees in a storm. He said Ebenezer was not willing to fix it and that was the one and only dealing he had with him."

"Did he write the note?" Ettie asked.

Kelly clamped his lips together the way he normally did when he didn't want to tell them more. They were only there for him to get information, and not the other way around. He only ever told them just enough. Kelly shook his head. "They said not, and Jack Simpson swears he didn't write it. He claims he had no need or reason to harm him. Now, according to your friend, Helga, Ebenezer had no relatives or close friends."

"None that we can think of. He probably had distant relatives and there is a lady in the community by the name of Ruth Esh, who keeps all the genealogical records, so she'd know."

"Where can I find her?" Kelly asked.

Ettie pulled her mouth to one side, thinking how the Amish were often reluctant to talk with outsiders. "Maybe we should speak with her first."

"Yes, you're quite right. She probably would only shut the door in my face. I've had that happen to me more times than I can count. Amish people have done that to me before. No offense."

"None taken," Elsa-May said with a laugh.

"If you wouldn't mind talking to her, I'd appreciate it."

"We'll do that first thing tomorrow. We've already had a big day."

"I understand. I'll find someone to drive you home."

Ettie's face lit up. It would save them money on a taxi fare. "Would you?"

He smiled, picked up the phone and they listened while he arranged for a young officer to take them home.

"Thank you." Ettie pushed herself to her feet. "We'll find out what we can and get back to you. When will the body be released?"

"I'll tell you the same thing I told your bishop. Possibly tomorrow." He bounded to his feet.

"Do you have leads?"

He narrowed his eyes. "We're working on half a dozen or so."

CHAPTER 5

ONCE THEY WERE BACK HOME and sitting in front of a toasty fire, Ettie racked her brain to remember all she could about Ebenezer. Meanwhile, Elsa-May sat with a black shawl over her shoulders, knitting as always.

"I'm upset with Kelly for keeping things from us."

"How do you know he is?" Elsa-May looked over the top of her glasses.

"He said he was working on leads, so what are they? How can we help him if he keeps us in the dark?"

"I don't know, Ettie. Might I remind you, I did advise you to stay out of this one?"

Ettie didn't catch that—she wasn't listening. "From what I can remember, Ebenezer came from another community. He didn't grow up here. I first remember him around the time my *kinskinner* were being born."

"Hmm." Elsa-May's eyes darted to the ceiling. "Around thirty to forty years ago."

"I guess that's about right and he would've been around seventy, so that means he arrived in this community when he was thirtyish. Do you remember him before that? If he was here we would know his parents."

"I vaguely recall he arrived here by himself."

Ettie was not going to rely on her sister's recollections when she'd forgotten about him altogether. "We'll find out for sure when we see Ruth. She'll know."

"Try to put it out of your mind and talk about something else."

Ettie looked down at Snowy who'd crawled out of his dog bed and had positioned himself on the couch next to her. "What do you think, Snowy?"

Snowy's eyes stayed closed and only his ears twitched on hearing his name.

It was hard for Ettie not to talk about all the questions racing through her mind. If Ebenezer was killed, it could've been that he had made an enemy out of someone in his younger years, and that could've been why he moved to their community. The enemy would've had a good long memory, though. Ettie giggled out loud at the sort-of-rhyme. *Enemy with a memory.*

"What's funny?"

"Nothing." Elsa-May wouldn't have found it amusing. Few things amused her these days.

"I've been meaning to ask you. What did you mean about Ebenezer not allowing the children to take a shortcut?"

Ettie rolled her eyes. "You said you remembered. It was the Bilicky *kinner.* "I think it was Jennifer who mentioned that there was some fuss about him not allowing the Bilicky children through the property as a shortcut to their friends' house. Then the bishop got involved and had to talk Ebenezer into allowing the children through."

"Who lived further out than Ebenezer, besides Helga and Levi?"

"Reg and Liz Bilicky. They had the dairy farm when their *kinner* were younger. They've sold it now."

"Why wouldn't he allow them through?"

"I don't know. You could've asked him but now we'll never know."

"I think I remember the whole thing now that you told me."

Ette shook her head. "Don't say you remember something next time when you don't."

"Can't we stay off that subject for tonight? Otherwise, I won't be able to go to sleep. I'll imagine someone coming for us."

"Oh, sorry. I didn't know that was the reason." Ettie stroked Snowy who was snuggled up on the couch beside her. "You'll protect us if someone comes in the *haus* tonight, won't you, Snowy?"

"What do you think, Ettie? He's suddenly going to triple in size and grow fangs? He's only a little dog. He won't be able to fend off our attackers." Elsa-May picked up her knitting.

Ettie chuckled, knowing if anything like that were to happen, Snowy would run under the bed to hide leaving the humans to fend for themselves.

"It's no use now," Elsa-May grumbled. "You've got me thinking about Ebenezer again." She stared at Ettie until Ettie shrugged her shoulders.

Elsa-May sighed. "All right. I know I can't stop thinking about it."

The fact that Elsa-May was scared troubled Ettie. Should she be worried too? "Are you serious about being scared?"

"I wouldn't say I'm terrified, but we're two old women living on our own. And don't forget what happened next door and that we were nearly killed because of it."

Ettie grimaced. "It'll take me a while to forget that."

"Let's talk about something else before we go to bed, so we go to sleep with good thoughts in our heads."

Ettie sneezed and managed to catch it with her handkerchief.

"You're not coming down with a cold, are you?"

"I don't think so."

"Keep warm. We'll need all our strength for when we visit Ruth tomorrow."

CHAPTER 6

THE NEXT MORNING, Elsa-May and Ettie were on their way out the door to see Ruth Esh when they were faced with Elsa-May's granddaughter, Becky, along with Elsa-May's great granddaughter, Ivy.

"This is a nice surprise," Elsa-May said.

"You're on your way somewhere?"

"Just to visit Ruth Esh."

"Would you mind taking Ivy along with you?"

"Hello, *Mammi.*" Ivy wrapped her arms around Elsa-May.

"Hello, Ivy. Are you ill?"

Ivy finished hugging Elsa-May and then hugged Ettie.

As she gave a hug to Elsa-May and then to Ettie, Becky said, *"Nee,* she's not ill. it's just that … it's just that I have some things to do and it would be faster for me if I didn't take Ivy with me."

Elsa-May hesitated and looked over at Ettie.

Becky added, "I've got errands. If I had anyone else to help me, I wouldn't be here. She's no trouble, really."

"This is a surprise, Ivy. A nice one though. I think we could take her with us, Elsa-May."

"*Jah,* we could, and it's always nice to spend time with you, Ivy."

"I love coming here and playing with Snowy. And I don't mind going out somewhere either. I love it because you go places in taxis. Cars are so much faster than buggies. It takes hardly any time at all to get places." Ivy turned around and looked at her mother.

"*Wunderbaar.* I'll be back mid-afternoon. Will you be home by then?"

"We can deliver her back to you," Elsa-May said.

"Are you sure?"

"*Jah.*"

"Okay." Becky put both hands on Ivy's shoulders. "You be a good girl now, you hear?"

"*Jah, Mamm.* I'll be good."

The three of them watched from the porch while Becky hurried back to her buggy.

"Maybe we should leave seeing Ruth for another day, Ettie. We can't drag Ivy with us everywhere."

"You can so. I'll be good," Ivy assured them.

"I know you will, but it won't be much fun for you."

As they moved back inside, Snowy ran over and sniffed Ivy's feet. "He's smelling my dogs on me. Hello, Snowy." Ivy leaned down and picked Snowy up. "He's heavy."

"Be careful," Elsa-May warned.

"Put him over on the couch," Ettie told her.

Ivy sat down on the couch with the dog on her knee. "I'd like to go out somewhere, *Mammi.* Pleeease?"

"I'm only concerned for you, that's all."

"It's settled then. I'm coming with you."

Elsa-May pulled a face as she sat down in her chair. "What do you think, Ettie?"

Ettie sat next to Ivy. "If she doesn't mind, let's move along with our plans."

"Goodie!"

"*Ach,* don't squeal so, Ivy."

"Sorry, *Mammi.*"

"I'll do those breakfast dishes before we go."

"*Denke,* Ettie."

Ettie left Elsa-May with her chubby-cheeked great granddaughter and listened in on their conversation from the kitchen.

"*Mammi,* would you rather break your leg or your arm?"

"Neither."

"You have to choose one."

"Do I?"

Ivy nodded and then stared at her wide-eyed waiting for a response.

"My arm because then I could still walk."

"Would you rather have all your teeth fall out or Snowy get run over by a car?"

Elsa-May gasped. "Neither."

"*Mammi,* I told you that you have to choose one. That's how the game works."

"Where do you get all these ideas from?" Elsa-May asked.

Ettie had overheard the whole thing and chuckled to herself.

"Just out of my head. Would you rather ..."

"No more of those questions, *denke*. Let's talk about something else."

"Tell me some stories about you and Aunt Ettie when you were younger?"

"Ah, there are so many stories." Elsa-May replied.

"I know. *Mamm* tells me all the stories her *mamm* told her about when you were little."

"What's your favorite?"

"I'll try to think of one, if you're quiet for a little while," Ivy said, trying to sound like an adult.

When Ivy asked another 'would you rather' question, Ettie realized why her mother suddenly had urgent matters she had to see about. Ettie drained the water from the sink, wiped down all the countertops, and then dried off her hands on a hand towel. Now they were ready to leave.

Ettie walked out into the living room. "Everyone ready?"

They all pulled on their thick black coats and their over-bonnets, and huddled together as they walked to the shanty at the end of the road to call a taxi.

Once they had made the call, they stood shivering. "I hope it won't be long," Elsa-May said.

Ettie moved from one foot to the other to warm herself. "We should've told them the address of our *haus* and waited there in the warmth."

Ivy took a deep breath. "Would you rather—"

"There's the taxi now." Elsa-May pointed into the distance.

Ivy turned around and had a good look. "Where? I don't see it?"

"Oh, my mistake. Anyway, how old are you now, Ivy?"

"Seven. I just had my birthday. You were there at the *haus* for my birthday dinner."

"That's right, I was."

"Did you forget that already, *Mammi?*"

"When people get old their memories sometimes fade," Elsa-May said.

"You can remember back to when you were a girl, *Mammi,* and that was way back in the olden days. Who's the oldest, you or Aunt Ettie? It's you isn't it, *Mammi?* And how old are you?"

"Very old," Elsa-May said.

"I know that, but what number are you?"

"It's a very large number," Ettie said.

"Well, what is it? And what about you, Aunt Ettie? You've got to be really old too."

"Ah, here's the taxi," Ettie said, never more pleased to see one and it wasn't because the December wind was biting into her cheeks.

On the way to Ruth's place, Ivy forgot her questions, and only remembered them when the taxi drove through the front gate of the property.

"Who's the oldest out of you two?" Ivy asked once again.

"Your great *grossmammi's* the oldest."

"That's right. That's what *mamm* told me."

"Where was your *mamm* going today?" Ettie asked.

"She said she needed some peace and quiet."

Elsa-May said to Ivy, "I only hope Ruth's home after all this. Ivy, you can't talk while we're here. We've got some important questions to ask Mrs. Esh."

"What if she asks how I am, or asks me if I'm having a

nice day? Oh, and everyone always asks me how old I am and how I like *schul*. I'd rather not talk about that."

"You can answer those kinds of questions. Wait a minute. Why aren't you at *schul?*"

"I felt a little off." When a smile twigged around Ivy's lips, Ettie knew she had just wanted a day without school. "What if—"

Ettie cut Ivy off. "You can answer anything Mrs. Esh asks you. But with short answers only. How's that?"

"Okay."

"You two stay here in the warmth of the car, and I'll see if Ruth's home." Ettie looked up at the driver. "Is that okay?"

"Sure."

Ettie didn't have to wait long after she knocked on the door. Ruth pulled it open, and stood there smiling. "It's nice to see you! Come in out of the cold."

"*Denke.* I have Elsa-May here with Ivy. We wanted to ask you some questions about Ebenezer."

"*Jah,* bring them in."

Ettie stepped to the edge of the porch and beckoned them in.

CHAPTER 7

Ivy walked alongside of Elsa-May as Ruth ushered them into the living room and sat them in front of the fire. Ettie was nearly overwhelmed by a musty odor and figured it was coming from the boxes that lined one wall of the living room. "What's in the boxes?"

"All my records for this community. I have everything my *grossmammi* passed down to me. I had it in the other room, but when we had that storm weeks ago, the roof leaked onto some of the boxes. I had Jacob help me move them all here. The fire will help dry them out."

"That's dreadful. They could've all been destroyed."

"I know, but they weren't and they'll dry off. Only the boxes got a little damp. You all look like you need a hot drink. What about some hot milk and cookies for you, Ivy?"

"*Denke.* I'd like that."

"*Nee*, don't go to any trouble, Ruth."

Ruth shook her head. "It's no trouble. I'll make us a pot of hot tea too."

"I'll help you," Ettie said, pushing herself to her feet.

"Is THERE anything you can tell us about Ebenezer?" Ettie asked once they were all seated with tea and cookies.

"It was a dreadful thing to happen."

"What happened?" Ivy said with cookie crumbs spilling out of her mouth.

Elsa-May frowned at her and brushed the crumbs off her face. "Mind your manners, Ivy."

"It's best you don't know," Ettie told Ivy, knowing she would've already heard about it.

"Oh, *that* man." Ivy nodded solemnly.

"That's right," Elsa-May said. "Now put that right out of your mind."

Ivy reached forward and took another cookie, having finished the first with haste.

Ruth continued, "He came to this community when he was ...he had to have been in his mid-twenties I'd say."

"Do you know where he came from?" Elsa-May asked.

"He came from Divine Creek community. It no longer exists. All our friends have moved on to live elsewhere. He was one of the founding members. That's what he told me when I asked him. I remember it as clear as you're both sitting here."

"Any family?"

"*Nee,* but I haven't finished yet. There's something else I must tell you, something odd. Back at the time, I wrote to the bishop from Divine Creek because a good genealogist verifies everything and he said he didn't know anyone by the name of Ebenezer Fuller."

"That's odd. Very odd. Didn't you find that strange at the time?"

Ruth shook her head. "I thought he'd been shunned and that it was the bishop's choice to deny knowledge of him until he was back in the fold."

"Did you say anything to our bishop about that?" Ettie asked.

"*Nee.* It wasn't my business to interfere. I try to stay out of trouble. You can't hide from *Gott.* If Ebenezer had done something, our bishop would've found out sooner or later."

Elsa-May eyed Ettie. "I think some of us could learn from that attitude."

"Is there anything, anything at all, you can tell us about Ebenezer? You see, we don't know much about him and Elsa-May even thought he'd died because we hadn't seen him around in so long."

Ruth turned and swept a hand toward her boxes of notes and papers. "All I know is what these tell me, and there's nothing there about Ebenezer. I'm sorry I can't be of more help."

"*Denke,* Ruth. You've been more help than you know."

"I try. I'm not used to turning people away without answering their questions. I've failed to do my job." She bit her lip. "I should've delved into things further back then, but nothing like that had happened before, and I didn't want to make any trouble for Ebenezer. I thought he was trying to make a new start for himself. If he was turned away from this community, he might've fallen by the wayside." She stared at Ettie. "Nearly everybody in this community has been traceable back many generations and even back to the old country."

Elsa-May patted her on her shoulder. "You've done a good job and you continue to do so."

"Do you think so?"

"We do," Ettie said. "Now we must go and leave you to your record-keeping in peace."

"I do have quite a bit of correspondence to get through today."

"I'll call for a taxi, and then we'll leave you to it."

When they heard a car arrive, they donned their coats and bonnets, said their goodbyes and walked out to their taxi.

Elsa-May said to Ettie. "I know that look. What were you thinking about? Did she say something I missed?"

"Divine Creek, Elsa-May."

"And? Should that mean something to me?"

"Our cousin, Deirdre once lived in Divine Creek."

"Where's she living now?"

"Walnut Creek. I got a letter from her a few weeks ago. I haven't written back yet, but I shall do so tonight. I'll ask her about Ebenezer and see what she says."

"Good idea, Ettie."

"*Denke.* It'll be interesting—if she remembers him."

"Should we tell Kelly what we learned just now?"

"*Nee.* We learned nothing."

"Then we should call and tell him that."

Ettie sighed and then had to agree with her sister.

"CAN I TALK NOW?" Ivy asked once they had gone a short distance in the taxi.

Elsa-May smiled. "Of course you can, and you were very well-behaved back there."

"*Denke.* Now, Aunt Ettie, would you rather be stabbed or shot?"

Ettie opened her mouth in shock and regretted having had Ivy around talk of Ebenezer.

Elsa-May said, "Ivy, you'll have to stop asking those questions."

"Why?"

"Because they're gruesome."

"And you don't give very good choices. One's just as bad as the other," Ettie said.

"Not really. Depending on where you get shot."

"Enough, Ivy!"

Ivy shuddered at Elsa-May's reprimand. "Sorry." Then she looked out the window for the rest of the journey. Ettie felt sorry for young Ivy, but she couldn't go around asking people those sorts of questions.

"We've got a little time before we take you back home, Ivy. How about a treat for you?"

"What kind of a treat?"

"We'll take you to a café and you can have a chocolate milkshake and whatever else you'd like to eat."

"For real?" The light was back in Ivy's blue eyes.

Elsa-May chuckled. *"Jah,* for real."

"I'd love that. *Mamm* never goes to those places. She says that we eat at home and it costs too much to eat at those places and she always says we have food at home. I'm sure everyone else has food at their homes too. Maybe they can't cook. Or, maybe they can't be bothered."

"That's why it's a treat," Ettie said.

· · ·

Once Elsa-May and Ettie were at their favorite coffee shop, Ivy picked up the edge of the tablecloth. "This is nice. Do we have to wash the dishes after we eat?"

"Someone else does that."

Ivy's eyes widened. "I'd like to eat here all the time."

Ettie and Elsa-May chuckled. "It is nice to get a rest from the chores," said Ettie.

"When I grow up I'm going to come back and eat here all the time."

"It might get a little expensive."

"We'll see." Ivy's face beamed.

When they were home after Ivy had been delivered back to her mother, Ettie set about writing to their cousin, hoping Deirdre might recall Ebenezer. Ettie hadn't gotten far into her letter, when she looked across at Elsa-May. "Divine Creek and now she lives in Walnut Creek."

"Perhaps she's following all the creeks." Elsa-May chuckled. "She might have a boat."

"Possibly." Ettie giggled at the thought. "I hope this letter brings news of Ebenezer."

"It would be her letter returning that would bring news because your letter is asking the questions."

Ettie clamped her lips together and kept quiet. Elsa-May was overly precise at times, annoyingly so. It was a trait she'd gotten from their father.

CHAPTER 8

"Ettie, they're here!"

"Coming!" Ettie was in her bedroom putting pins into the plaits against her head. After she anchored the last pin, she carefully placed her white prayer *kapp* on her head and tied the strings under her neck. When she walked out of her room, she saw Elsa-May at the front door, fuming.

"Why are we always waiting for you on a Sunday morning?"

"You're not."

Elsa-May was already dressed in her black coat and over-bonnet. "You don't even have your coat on."

Ettie grabbed her coat. "See? Now I'm ready. You start walking to the buggy and I'll be there before you."

Elsa-May shook her head once again, and walked out of the house. When she'd gotten to the first step, Ettie passed by her and then reached the gate before her.

"You'll end up slipping on the path if you don't be careful," Elsa-May called out.

Ettie reached Ava and Jeremiah's buggy first, and greeted them as she slid into the back seat. To make room for Elsa-May, she moved closer to the baby who was asleep strapped into his seat.

Elsa-May sat beside her and no sooner said hello to Ava and Jeremiah than, she said to Ettie, "You keep me waiting, Ettie, and then you're first to the buggy to make it look like I was the one who kept Ava and Jeremiah waiting."

Jeremiah had already moved the buggy away. "It doesn't matter. No one needs to argue."

"It's not me it's her," Ettie said.

"And you sat next to Aaron when you knew I wanted to," Elsa-May whispered to Ettie.

Ettie ignored Elsa-May. "You two heard about Ebenezer?"

"We sure have," Ava said swivelling to face them.

"Don't start gossiping," Jeremiah said.

"We're not," Ava answered. "We're just talking."

"Talk to you about it a bit later then," Elsa-May said smugly.

"Do you know who did it?" Ava asked.

"Not yet, but there was a nurse who came to his *haus* when we were there."

"After he died?" asked Ava.

"*Jah,* the day after."

"What were you doing at his *haus?*" Jeremiah asked. "I didn't know you knew him well."

"Well enough," Elsa-May answered.

"What about the nurse?" Ava asked.

"Ettie thinks there's something funny about her," Elsa-May said.

"Like what, Ettie?"

"I can't quite put my finger on it." She didn't want to talk much in front of Jeremiah.

"Let's talk about something else, shall we?" Jeremiah said. "Let the police look after it."

"We are," Elsa-May said.

"Have you got new neighbors yet?" Jeremiah asked.

Ettie chuckled. "Don't get Elsa-May started talking about that."

"Me? You're the one worried about it. I didn't mind if we never get neighbors. Only thing is, it's a waste to see it empty."

"The King family is looking for a new place, I heard," Jeremiah said.

"*Nee*, it's not big enough for them. They need a big home."

"You had a nice man living next door to you before, and he gave you Snowy from the animal shelter," Ava said.

"That's true. We're praying for some nice neighbors."

"It could be possible. But what kind of person would want to live in a place where someone's been murdered?" Elsa-May asked.

"There are people who wouldn't be bothered by that," Jeremiah said. "It wouldn't bother me. They got the person who did it, didn't they?"

"That's right. They did. It's a story to tell you on another day if you don't already know it."

Jeremiah made no comment.

When Jeremiah parked the buggy at the house where the meeting was being held, they unbuckled the baby and lifted him out of the car seat. He didn't wake, and Ava took him in her arms and walked with Ettie and Elsa-May to the bishop's house while Jeremiah secured the horse and buggy.

"Tell me quickly now, what's really going on?" Ava asked as they walked.

"I didn't want to say this in front of Jeremiah, but the day we were there the house had crime scene tape around it."

"I heard he was found outside behind his barn."

"He was, but still, they had the tape around the *haus* too as well as the yard."

Elsa-May added, "We knew the detectives had already been looking for their clues and whatnot."

"So, we slipped under the tape and went into the house looking for something they might've missed. We wouldn't have, if we hadn't seen them leave."

"And what did you find?"

"It wasn't so much about what we found. We were only there five minutes when the nurse arrived. We watched her from the window and she slipped straight under the tape and into the house."

"What happened?"

"Not much. Ettie opened the door, we said hello, and she didn't even say why she was there."

"That is a little weird."

"It immediately made me suspicious of her. I wondered if she wasn't a nurse, but apparently she is a real one. We saw where she worked. And she came to see him every few weeks, she said."

"She drove us into town. She wanted to know when the funeral was. I suppose someone will tell her when it's arranged."

"What's her name?"

"Patricia Stuart."

"I'll see what I can find out about her from the local library. I'll go onto the computer."

"Don't trouble yourself with that. I'm sure Jeremiah wouldn't like you helping us now that you've got the *boppli* to look after."

"I don't mind. I truly don't mind and anyway *Mamm* insists on looking after him two days a week and then I'm free to do whatever I want."

"I'd rather you not get involved if you don't mind, Ava."

"*Jah,*" Ettie agreed. "We don't want to upset Jeremiah."

They had arrived at the front door of the bishop's house. "We'll talk later," Ava whispered.

WHEN THE PREACHING WAS OVER, and it was meal time, Ettie sought out the bishop.

"Hello, Bishop John. I have a question for you. How did you know how to reach Ebenezer's nurse?"

"You spoke with her?"

Ettie nodded, hoping he didn't ask where, or when.

"Last time I visited him she was there and I took down her phone number. I thought it was best."

Ettie slowly nodded. "It was good that you did."

"It was a precaution in case he fell ill. He wasn't a well man."

"We didn't know he was ill."

"Perhaps he wasn't, but he didn't seem vibrant. He was always sorrowful about things and I've noticed that people who feel that way get ill more often."

"Do you know when the funeral will be?"

"We wanted it Wednesday, but we don't know when they'll be finished with his body. I'm guessing it'll have to be Friday now."

"Do you know anyone who was upset with Ebenezer?"

Bishop John rubbed his neck. "He ruffled a few feathers trying to fit in with everyone when he first got here, but then he settled in." He looked around the crowd of people in his house. "I can't think of a person who was upset with him. He was gruff and people dropped off visiting him. Mary and I visited him as often as we could, but we couldn't be there often enough."

"Was it only Helga and Levi you asked to watch him?"

The bishop frowned. "I didn't ask anyone to do any such thing."

Ettie took a small step closer to him. "You didn't ask them to keep an eye on him since they lived close?"

He shook his head. "I wouldn't have, because Levi and Ebenezer didn't get along too well. Mary and I visited Ebenezer every fortnight. He wasn't talkative for someone who lived alone. He was a loner, for certain." The bishop shook his head.

"Yes. And why was the nurse visiting him if he wasn't ill?"

"I asked her that and she talked about a local program that's been set up and Ebenezer was happy to be part of it."

"She said the same to us. Has anybody contacted you— any of Ebenezer's close relatives or friends?"

The bishop shook his head. "There seems to be no one. No one's come forward to say that they were related to him."

. . .

SOMEONE WALKED UP and stood behind the bishop, clearly waiting to talk with him. The bishop looked over his shoulder at the man, and then looked back at Ettie and her sister. "I'll talk to you both later."

"Okay."

When the bishop turned away from them, Ettie spotted Ivy. "There's Ivy."

"*Ach.* She might ask us those dreadful things again."

"Quick! Before she sees us, let's go help in the kitchen."

They hurried back toward the kitchen to help with the food preparations.

Once they were safely away from Ivy's line of sight, Elsa-May asked, "What do you think now, Ettie?"

"I don't know what to think. Did Helga lie to us or was she only confused?"

"She wouldn't have lied. Surely not. Do you think you're wrong about the nurse?"

"I think we can safely say she was a nurse. That's all we know for certain about her. I would like to know more about her."

Just before they reached the kitchen, Ava stopped them. "What are you two cooking up?"

"We're talking about the nurse," Elsa-May whispered

"I'll see what I can find out about her. What was her name again?"

"Patricia Stuart. We don't know which spelling for the last name, though," said Ettie, "whether it's a 'u' or 'e-w' in the middle."

"That won't matter much. It's quick to look for her under both spellings."

"I doubt you'll find out anything," said Elsa-May.

"But I can try. I'll go to the library tomorrow and use the computer."

Elsa-May put her hand on Ava's. "Don't go to all that trouble. Jeremiah won't like it."

"He won't mind."

"I think he will."

"He doesn't mind fact-finding. He just doesn't like it when he thinks we're gossiping. Trust me, it's okay that I do research."

"The police might come up with something soon. Maybe a fingerprint or something," Ettie muttered, hoping they would.

"Did Kelly say he was coming to the funeral?"

"He said he'd be at the cemetery."

When more people came into the kitchen, they had to stop talking. While they helped out with the food, Ettie was lost in thoughts about the two different stories the bishop had told about Ebenezer. Helga never mentioned Ebenezer and her husband not getting along, but that might've been because no one got along terribly well with Ebenezer. And Helga had clearly said Bishop John asked her and her husband to look after Ebenezer, but the bishop denied ever doing any such thing.

CHAPTER 9

On Monday, Elsa-May woke up with a head cold, so Ettie had to abandon her plans of investigating and she stayed home and looked after her sister.

It was afternoon when Ava arrived at their house with news.

"The body has been released," was the first thing she said when Ettie opened the door.

"Come inside. Elsa-May's not feeling very well."

"Oh, what's wrong?" Ava rushed over to Elsa-May who was lying on the couch.

"She's got a head cold. It's nothing serious."

"It feels it," Elsa-May groaned. "Ettie's been looking after me quite well."

Ettie shrugged her shoulders. "There's been nothing else to do."

Ava sat down on a chair opposite the couch, while Ettie sat in Elsa-May's usual chair.

"The funeral's on Wednesday," Ava told them.

"Wednesday? They're not wasting any time. Bishop John thought they'd have to wait until Friday."

"He doesn't have any one coming from far away, so Wednesday's the day. I also found out that the nurse, Patricia—and S-t-u-a-r-t is the correct spelling—got left a sum of money by one of her elderly patients. She said she was giving it to charity."

Elsa-May half sat up. "You talked with her?"

"*Nee.*"

"How did you find that out?" Elsa-May asked as she lowered herself back onto her pillows.

"There was an article in one of the newspaper about it. I went to the library like I said, and I found out all this from the Internet. There was some kind of expose on nurses who inherited money from sick and elderly patients, and she was named."

"I don't think Ebenezer had any money, did he?" Ettie asked.

"I'm not sure. I saw the bishop in town when I was coming out of the library. He's having everyone spread the word about the funeral, and he asked me if I could let you know. I have to go, but we'll collect you for the funeral, *jah?*"

"Please, Ava."

"That would be lovely, *denke.*"

"I hope you'll be feeling much better by then, Elsa-May."

"She'll be fine."

Elsa-May's mouth turned down at the corners. "I hope so."

When Ava left, Ettie sat opposite Elsa-May. "I'm going to ask for the nurse's phone number if she's at the funeral.

I won't talk to her about anything there, but I want some answers."

"Just ask her at the funeral. You don't have to make a big thing out of it."

"*Nee.*"

"Please yourself. You usually do. May I have another bowl of soup?"

"Sure. I just hope you're better by Wednesday."

ON TUESDAY ELSA-MAY was a little better and when Wednesday came, she was well enough to attend the funeral. The sisters were collected by Ava and Jeremiah and driven to the bishop's house for the viewing prior to the burial.

ONCE INSIDE THE bishop's house, Ettie stood next to Elsa-May at the back of the room observing everyone. "There aren't many people here from outside this community."

"That's unusual. If it was anyone else's funeral we'd have people from far and wide."

"He had no friends outside of this community."

"And I'd say acquaintances rather than friends," Elsa-May corrected Ettie.

"*Jah.* That's so sad." Ettie shook her head. "If only we had known, we might've been able to extend a hand of friendship."

"Well it's too late for that now."

Ettie's gaze drifted to the coffin and she wondered who was looking after Ebenezer's house now that he'd

SAMANTHA PRICE

died. Had he left the bishop in charge of his will and those matters?

That was something Ettie had to find out. If he had a will, someone could've benefited by his death. She'd slipped up this time. That was normally the first thing she found out. The detective would know, but he'd told her nothing.

"Elsa-May, did Ebenezer have a lot of money?"

"How would I know?"

"Who would know?"

"Maybe the bishop."

Ettie nodded. "We have to find out from him before we go home today."

"Probably the best time for that would be at the grave-yard when everybody's leaving. What do you think?"

"That sounds like a good idea."

It wasn't long before everyone was in their buggies and in single file following the custom-made funeral buggy to the graveyard.

Ava stayed in the buggy with Aaron, who had fallen asleep. Ettie and Elsa-May, with Jeremiah holding an arm each, made their way to the freshly dug grave.

Jeremiah looked up at the gray sky. "Why does it always rain at funerals?"

"I hope *Gott* holds back the rain until we're ready to leave."

Ettie said, "It seems Ebenezer is showing his disapproval over how he died."

"Oh, Ettie, you do talk a lot of rot." Elsa-May shook her head. "He wouldn't be able to control the weather from where he is."

Ettie chuckled. "Sometimes I just like to think about things like that."

"I have no idea how your mind clicks, Ettie."

Jeremiah butted in to their conversation, "Do you two have to argue all the time?"

"We don't. Not all the time," Elsa-May said to her grandson.

"I also don't like Ava getting involved with these things."

"We try to keep her out of things, but she's strong minded."

Jeremiah chuckled. "I know what you mean. She certainly is that."

"Don't worry, Jeremiah, I'm keeping a very close eye on her," Elsa-May said.

"Somehow, that doesn't make me feel much better. With the two of you around, there always seems to be weird goings-on."

Ettie and Elsa-May chuckled, and then Elsa-May patted Jeremiah on his shoulder. "We have no idea what you're talking about."

Jeremiah sighed. "I guess I'm better off not knowing."

"That's right. You're better kept in the dark."

CHAPTER 10

As they stood at the grave waiting for the crowd to move from the buggies to gather around, Ettie noticed *Englischers.*

Elsa-May saw them too, nodding in their direction.

"Ettie, look over there."

"I see them. I'll say hello and find out who they are." She walked right over to an older man standing with an arm around a woman about his age, and a young man standing with them. "Hello, may I ask how you knew Ebenezer?"

"My wife and I live next door to him. We've got the cottonseed farm."

Ettie realized they owned the fields she and her sister had walked through to get to Ebenezer's house. She turned her attention to the boy. "And do you live next door as well?" He could've been the right age to be their son.

"No, I'm not related. I just met these people today. We

kind of gravitated together because we're the only people here who aren't Amish." He glanced over at the crowd.

"I see." Ettie noticed the man was holding on to his wife almost as though he were holding her up. Her eyes were red-rimmed and then Ettie saw her hands were hidden under a shawl. "And how did you know Ebenezer?" she asked the young man.

"I delivered his food once a week. He liked his fruit. And he was very particular about his fruit. It couldn't be under-ripe or over-ripe."

"You knew him well?"

"We did get along together after a while. I found him gruff to start with but then we became almost like friends."

Ettie introduced herself and they did the same. The neighbors were Jack and Blythe Simpson, and the young man's name was Pete Ross. When she said goodbye to them and was heading back to Elsa-May and Jeremiah, she spied the nurse walking toward the crowd and changed direction to meet her.

Before Ettie could say a thing, Patricia blurted out, "My car wouldn't start. I thought I'd be late and miss it all."

"You're just in time," Ettie told her. "Would you mind if I arrange a time to speak with you about Ebenezer?"

She scrunched her brows and stared at Ettie. "About what?"

"I have some questions but today's not the right time. Could we perhaps meet in a café near your work?"

"Okay, but I can't tomorrow."

"Friday, then?"

She hesitated and smiled awkwardly. "Wait, I can do it

tomorrow. It's my day off, but I'll be out that way. I can meet you somewhere in town. What about twelve o'clock?"

"That sounds perfect. Where shall we meet?"

"There is a café two doors down from the clinic. It's got a green and white awning."

"I know the one. I've seen it before. I'll see you there." Ettie hurried back to Elsa-May while the nurse stayed close to the other Englischers.

"What did you find out?" Elsa-May whispered.

"They're the neighbors, the older two, and the boy who delivered the fruit."

"Delivered the fruit?"

"He got his food delivered every week and that was the boy who did it. Sounds like they became friends."

"Friends? What would an old man have in common with such a young man?"

"Maybe he was some kind of mentor for the young boy."

"I find that hard to believe."

Ettie scrunched her shoulders. "That's what he said, that they were friends, I mean."

The bishop called out and asked everyone to gather closer, and then he began. He opened his bible and read a passage of scripture in High German. It was from John 14.

Let not your heart be troubled: ye believe in God, believe also in me.

In my Father's house are many mansions: if it were not so, I would have told you. I go to prepare a place for you.

And if I go and prepare a place for you, I will come again, and receive you unto myself; that where I am, there ye may be also.

Then the bishop closed his bible and said a few words about this life being temporary, and how it was a blink of an eye compared with eternity. A lengthy prayer followed.

Ettie stole a sideways glance at Elsa-May knowing her sister was thinking about whether the next funeral would be her own. Normally, Elsa-May joked about that being the case, but at this funeral she'd said nothing of the kind.

On top of that, Christmas was close and Elsa-May always pointed out that this might be their last Christmas together. This time Elsa-May hadn't mentioned that either, but Ettie knew she would say it soon enough. Ettie closed her eyes and wondered what the last moments of Ebenezer's life had been like. Did he know the person who killed him, or was it a complete stranger? Detective Kelly said he had been stabbed in the back, so had Ebenezer even seen the person who'd taken his life? Had the person come at him and chased him, or was he attacked as he waited for that mystery person at the boundary fences.

"Amen," the bishop said just as a large droplet of rain landed on the end of Ettie's nose causing her to jump in fright.

"What is it?" Elsa-May whispered.

Ettie looked up to the sky wiping her nose with her coat sleeve. "I think I just felt rain."

At that very moment, rain poured from the sky causing everyone to scatter.

"*Gott* held the rain back, Ettie. Or do you think it was Ebenezer?" Elsa-May cackled, just as Jeremiah took off his coat and held it over their heads.

"Come on," he urged them. Together they hurried back to the buggy. By the time they got there, Jeremiah's white shirt was drenched and sticking to his skin. While they got into the buggy, Ava handed Jeremiah a blanket.

"Are you two okay?" she asked Ettie and Elsa-May.

"We're fine thanks to Jeremiah," Ettie said.

Jeremiah stated, "We'll take you straight home."

"*Nee,* we should go back to the bishop's *haus* with everyone else."

"I won't hear of it not with you being sick, *Mammi.* I'll take you home and start a fire for you. You both have to start looking after yourselves at your age."

"I'm fine! I'm not sick."

"Really? You look a little pale and you've got dark circles under your eyes."

Elsa-May opened her eyes wide and put a hand to her face.

Ava said, "We should go right home after that, too, Jeremiah. You're soaked to the skin and Aaron has been fussy all day."

"I won't argue with that."

WHEN THE SISTERS were finally alone in front of a warm fire, Ettie looked down at her feet in her fluffy slippers. Then she looked over at Elsa-May's feet in the slippers she'd knitted herself. Nearly everything of Elsa-May's was knitted.

"Do I still look sick to you?" Elsa-May asked.

"*Nee.* You look the same as always."

After a few more rows, Elsa-May said, "I just realized Kelly wasn't at the funeral."

"*Jah,* that is odd."

"Something must've come up."

"I wonder what. You stay in front of the fire and I'll heat some soup for us."

"*Denke,* Ettie."

"Tonight, we should go to bed early because we're meeting with the nurse tomorrow."

"We are?"

"Didn't I tell you?"

"*Nee,* you didn't."

"She agreed to meet with us. I said I had some questions I wanted to ask, so we're meeting her at lunchtime at a café."

Elsa-May sighed. "An early night sounds good to me."

CHAPTER 11

AFTER AN EARLY DINNER of soup and toast, Elsa-May and Ettie were back enjoying the warmth of the fire when they heard a knock on their door.

"Who could that be?" Elsa-May said.

"That'll be someone."

"Well, open the door and see *which* someone."

Ettie chuckled to herself as she headed to the door. When she opened it, she saw the handsome face of Gabriel Yoder. "Gabriel!"

"Hello, I have some good news. It's the best news I've had in years. Certainly the best news I've had today, since I spent most of it at the funeral. I never like going to funerals."

"We could use some good news," Elsa-May called out from her chair.

"We could indeed. Come in out of the cold."

Gabriel walked in, took off his coat and hat and Ettie took them and laid them on the side table near the door.

"Put the teakettle on, Ettie."

Gabriel raised his hands. *"Nee,* not for me. I'm fine. I've just come from the bishop's *haus* and I've had far too much to eat."

Ettie took him by the arm and guided him toward the couch and then she sat down while he remained standing.

"Tell us this good news, Gabriel."

"It's Selena Lehman. She finally returned one of my calls this morning and told me she's coming back! Remember her? She's Abner Troyer's granddaughter. Her mother ran away from the community, but Selena has one fond memory of visiting her *grossdaddi."*

"That's *wunderbaar.* Is the King family moving out of the *haus* her *grossdaddi* left for her?"

He lowered his tall frame onto the couch. *"Nee.* They're having trouble finding another place big enough for their family. Also, she doesn't get it officially until she's thirty or married."

"Humph. We slept four to a room in our day," Elsa-May said.

"That's the only thing holding her up from coming here. She won't force the Kings to leave, and she's sublet her apartment already and has to be out soon. She's asked me to find her a house. Can you imagine that? She's asked me!"

"That's ... exciting for you." Elsa-May grinned.

"She's the woman for me. I knew it the first time I saw her. *Gott* sent her to me. I prayed for him to go anywhere into the world and bring the right woman to me. Then she appeared."

"Is she joining us?" Ettie asked.

"Her words were, she might—might think about it." He stared at Ettie and then looked over at Elsa-May.

Elsa-May smiled at him and started another row of knitting. "You're quite fond of her I see."

"More than that. When she's around, I can smell the air and the trees. I can even feel the air on my cheeks when there's no breeze. It's like I come alive only when she's near." When neither of them commented he cleared his throat. "Have I come at a bad time?"

"*Nee*, we're just upset over Ebenezer."

"Ah, that's a loss. A sad loss to all."

"Did you know him well?" Ettie asked.

"I became close in the last few months after Selena's *grossdaddi* died. They were friends, the two of them."

"Really?" The fact Ebenezer had a friend was news to Ettie.

Elsa-May took off her glasses, folded them into the neckline of her dress, then popped her knitting into the bag by her feet. "Is that right?"

"*Jah*, I was there nearly every day since Selena's *grossdaddi* went to *Gott*. I missed one day and that was the day they found him."

"And what made you miss that day?" Ettie asked. "I heard he was missing for a couple of days."

"*Nee*, Ettie. He wasn't seen for a couple of days, by Helga. That didn't mean he was missing."

"He was never missing, Ettie."

"What prevented you going there that day?"

"Someone let my horses out."

"That's dreadful."

"I know. But I found them and they were safe, so there was no harm done."

"Who knew you visited him?" Elsa-May asked.

"I'm not sure. Everyone, I think."

"Did you see other people while you were there? Or do you know who else he was friendly with?"

"His nurse, Patricia, and Pete, the man who delivered the food. They were the main people I saw. He talked about the woman next door like she was a friend, but I never saw her."

"That's interesting. Do you know anyone who might've wished him harm?"

"*Nee.*"

"Why and how did you get to know him? He hadn't been to a meeting in years."

"Like I said, when Abner died, I missed him and gave it some thought about who else I might talk to so I could gain wisdom. I remembered Abner asked me to take him to Ebenezer's once, so I stopped by and Ebenezer and I had a good talk. I kept going back."

"And, did you gain wisdom?" Elsa-May asked.

"That's not for me to say." Gabriel chuckled. "What I found was a friend."

"Did he talk about anyone he didn't get along with?"

Slowly he shook his head. "Are you trying to find out who killed him?"

"*Jah*, and anything you could tell us might help. Anything at all that you might think of."

He shrugged his shoulders. "Isn't it better to leave things in *Gott's* hands rather than seek earthly justice?" He clasped his hands together in his lap and when neither lady answered his question, he said, "He was annoyed with his neighbors, or more accurately the neighbor man, but he never said why."

"Did he get along with the nurse?"

"He looked forward to her visits. She was often there."

"And, how often was that?"

"Once a week, I'd say. Not officially, but she'd often stop by to say hello when she was passing by. That's all I know. I wouldn't know who'd want the old man dead. If I can think of anything I'll let you know. Selena might be able to help. She was once a police officer."

Ettie shook her head, pretty sure all his conversations would come back around to Selena. "She wouldn't be able to find out any more than Detective Kelly, but *denke* anyway."

"It would give me an excuse to call her. I told her about Ebenezer already. I tell her everything."

Ettie saw stars in his eyes every time he mentioned Selena. She remembered back to when she was young and in love, and hoped Gabriel wasn't heading for a fall. After all, Selena had only said she 'might think about' joining the community. To Ettie, that did not sound hopeful.

"There is the *haus* next door. They can't sell it, so whoever is controlling ownership of it might consider leasing. What about that for Selena?"

"*Nee*, Elsa-May. I couldn't ask her to consider a *haus* where someone was murdered. *Denke* for the thought anyway. She loves my *haus*. I need to find her something like mine. Now, if she'd marry me we could both live there together." He threw his head back and laughed.

"That would be ideal, and she'd have to join us to marry you, of course."

"That's what I'm praying for. Have you seen her eyes?"

Elsa-May shook her head. "Haven't noticed."

Ettie shrugged her shoulders.

"They're the most amazing green you've ever seen. *Gott* took the best shades of the trees and the grass and sprinkled them into her eyes. Then he kissed her hair with shades of gold from the morning sun."

Ettie had to press her fingernail into the palm of her hand to stop herself from laughing.

Elsa-May cleared her throat. "She likes your *haus?*"

"Who wouldn't? It's delightful. I've made it into a home. I take care of it and clean it every day and keep it … well, clean. I'd make Selena a *wunderbaar* husband."

Elsa-May leaned forward. "I suppose you've told her that?"

"Of course."

Elsa-May giggled.

"My prayers are that one day we'll marry. Someday soon, she'll see I'm the only man for her."

Ettie wasn't sure what to say. She didn't want to ruin his hopes and dreams, but what if his love for Selena blinded him to single women within their community? "I hope you won't be disappointed."

"She's moving here, Ettie. My prayers are already working. He's heard them."

Ettie had to laugh at the silly grin on his face. He was a happy man to have around, but would Selena ever join their community? Or was it love's foolish dream?

"One thing happened that I thought was odd. The last time I saw him—Ebenezer—he seemed bothered by something."

Ettie leaned forward. "Did he say what was wrong?"

"*Nee.* I asked him if I'd done something to upset him and he said I hadn't. That's all he said."

"How was he acting?" Elsa-May asked.

"Like he was depressed. He was down about something."

. . .

WHEN GABRIEL LEFT, Ettie and Elsa-May sat back down in the living room after waving goodbye to him.

"What do you think about that, Elsa-May? Ebenezer was upset over something."

"It could've been anything. I'm more concerned about Gabriel's love for an outsider."

"It's unrequited love."

"Jah. Any warning we'd give him would go in one ear and out the other. Love is blind and it's also deaf."

Ettie giggled. "All his common sense has gone and he's the only one who can get himself through this and drag himself out the other side. It's safe for him to love someone whom he'll never marry. He's scared of marrying. That must be it."

"Ettie, you talk a lot of gibberish. He's in love with her, he's not scared of anything."

Ettie pursed her lips. Wasn't she allowed to have her own opinion? "Anyway, it's odd that he'd been to Ebenezer's every day, and yet Helga made no mention of him."

"Jah, I noticed that too. Either Helga wasn't telling us the full truth, or Gabriel wasn't. I think Helga is keeping things from us."

"Tomorrow we meet with Patricia, and then we'll know more. We could visit Helga after that."

Elsa-May nodded. "We'll do that."

CHAPTER 12

THE NEXT MORNING, Ettie's heart thumped hard when she saw Detective Kelly getting out of his car in front of their house. She studied Kelly's face to see if he was angry. She couldn't tell if he was or wasn't because he always wore that same grim face. Had he heard they'd arranged to meet the nurse? That was the thing that worried her. She flung open the door just as he stepped onto the porch.

His face softened into a rare smile. "I have a piece of information you might not know."

Immediately, Ettie was relieved. "Come inside and sit down."

Kelly followed Ettie, and nodded to Elsa-May who sat knitting in her usual chair. Kelly chose to sit on one of the wooden chairs that were lined up in a row opposite Ettie's spot, which was the couch.

"What is it that we might or might not know?" Ettie asked.

"It seems that the neighbors, Jack and Blythe Simpson, wanted to buy Ebenezer's land."

Ettie gasped. "How do you know that?"

He smirked. "I just asked the right people the right questions."

Ettie looked over at Elsa-May who seemed just as surprised. *Wouldn't Gabriel have known that?* Ettie wondered.

Elsa-May looked over the top of her glasses at him. "Who inherits Ebenezer's land and his house?"

"He left everything to your community."

Ettie's mouth fell open. "That's the first time we're hearing about this."

"Your bishop knew."

"That's something we didn't think to ask him, Ettie."

"Well, now you know." Kelly smiled.

"Do you think they killed him over something to do with the land?"

"Probably not because now they don't get the land."

"Unless the bishop sells it to them," Ettie said. "They might have a better chance now than when Ebenezer was living on the land. Where would he have gone if he sold?"

Kelly shook his head. "But still, it doesn't seem a valid motive to me. This was a crime of anger, not a carefully planned killing."

"That's right. That's what we thought. Ettie said—"

Ettie butted in, "So why was he killed? Someone got into an argument with him and it wasn't planned, is that what you think, Detective?"

"That, Mrs. Smith, is one of the things we're trying to ascertain."

"What about your forensic evidence?"

"Wait a moment; back up a minute," Elsa-May said. "He left the land and everything to the community?"

"That's right."

"What is it, Elsa-May?"

"In the back of my mind ... there's something there, but it's just not coming to the front."

"What?" Kelly asked.

"I don't know." Elsa-May continued on with her knitting without saying anything.

Ettie didn't place much store in whatever was in the back of her sister's mind since she hadn't remembered who Ebenezer was. She smiled privately, imagining the poor lost thought trying to meander its way out.

The detective rubbed his neck and Ettie knew he was bothered by something. Then he exhaled deeply. "I'm under a lot of pressure from higher up to get this case solved. I don't mind telling you I've got a higher than average record for closing cases, but if the media gets hold of this they can make it into a circus. That's why I need to wrap it up before fear spreads through the community, and I'm not talking about just the Amish community."

"We're doing all we can," Ettie said.

He nodded. "I know you are." He clasped his hands together and leaned forward. "Surely there are other people you can question and delve into things further?"

Ettie raised her eyebrows. "I did ask our cousin, Deirdre, from Divine Creek. I asked her if she knew about Ebenezer."

"Tell him the story, Ettie." Elsa-May rolled her eyes at her sister, and continued, "I'll tell him. When Ebenezer came to this community he told people he was from Divine Creek. Ruth Esh contacted the bishop of Divine Creek and asked him a few things about Ebenezer's background—his family and such. It was her job to do so. He wrote back informing her he'd never heard of him. Yet, Ebenezer had told Ruth that he was one of the founding members."

"Ebenezer told Ruth he was a founding member of the Divine Creek community of Amish people?"

"That's right and it was a lie."

Ettie cleared her throat. "You see, our cousin used to live in Divine Creek and now she doesn't."

"It no longer exists," said Elsa-May.

Then Ettie commented, "She lives in Walnut Creek now."

Detective Kelly's head was swiveling from one sister to the other.

Elsa-May laughed. "We thought it funny about her living in places that end in the word 'creek.'"

"And?" Detective Kelly asked, now looking at Ettie.

"And … what?"

"What did your cousin say? Does she know anything about Ebenezer? Their bishop said he wasn't from there, so does that mean he wasn't?"

Before Ettie could answer, Elsa-May said, "Ruth thought that Ebenezer might've been shunned at the time and that's why the bishop might've refused any knowledge of him. That's why Ettie wrote to our cousin."

He shook his head. "You wrote a letter? Snail mail style?"

"Yes." Ettie was pleased with herself until she saw Kelly continuing to scowl at her. "What's the matter?"

"Couldn't you have just called her? Don't most of you have phones in your barns or something?"

"She doesn't have a phone. I could've called her neighbor. I didn't think of that. I could've called her neighbor to deliver her a message. A message to write to me and let me know what she knew about one Ebenezer Fuller, but I would still have been waiting on a letter back since we don't have a phone either."

Kelly huffed. "Would you please do that Mrs. Smith? At least it would speed the process. I really need to find out who wanted the old man dead. He had nothing of value. As far as we know, nothing was stolen."

Elsa-May shook her head. "He wouldn't have had anything of value."

"It's a mystery all right, but one that is vital I solve, and sooner rather than later. Time is of the essence. I'd appreciate anything you two can do to help me out."

"We'll ask around more," Ettie said. "And I'll call my cousin's neighbor today."

"Thank you. It would be very much appreciated."

"Of course." Ettie leaned forward. "What do you think about the nurse?"

Kelly stared at her. "Patricia?"

"Yes—she was at the funeral."

"She's got nothing to do with it."

Ettie narrowed her eyes at him, wondering why he was so adamant.

"Did you check her background?" Elsa-May asked.

"More importantly, did you check her hands to see if she had cuts on them? She's always wearing gloves every time I've seen her."

"Most people do in this weather, Mrs. Smith. I don't have time for you to go barking up the wrong tree. Wait a minute, how many times have you seen her?"

Ettie gulped, but was saved by Elsa-May.

"You've checked into her background then?" Elsa-May asked once more.

He nodded and gave a grunt. That told Ettie he most likely hadn't checked too closely, otherwise, he would've said so with conviction. "I know you don't think there's anything suspicious about her, but I do. We also found out that a patient left her money. Ava found that out from the computer in the library."

"I know that already. When I was questioning Patricia, she came right out and told me. She was upfront about the whole thing. She had no idea the man was leaving her money and she donated it to charity."

"I see." Ettie remained quiet about her intended meeting with Patricia later in the day.

"Why do you think she's innocent? Do you think she's too beautiful to be a killer?"

Kelly went red in the cheeks at Elsa-May's question. "Murderers come in all shapes and sizes, but she doesn't fit the profile. And remember, Ebenezer didn't leave anything to her. He left it to the community." He wagged a finger at both of them. "I'm relying on you two to help. I know there's something you're both missing. Someone in the community must know more than they're letting on. There must be some clue, something you've missed. Someone must've had a falling out with him somewhere along the way. It wasn't a stranger. I've had enough experience on the force to know that."

Ettie slowly nodded knowing he was right. "All right, I'll get around and question as many people as I can."

"That's the idea." Kelly leaned back in the chair. "Now, how about a cup of hot tea? And perhaps a taste of some of your home-baked goodies?"

Elsa-May shook her head and jabbed her knitting needles into her ball of wool. "We don't have time. We have to get out and start questioning people, and that starts now."

He bounded to his feet. "I like the sound of that."

Ettie giggled. "We'll be back in touch as soon as we find out anything."

As they walked him to the front door, Elsa-May asked him the question from moments ago that he hadn't yet answered, "How are the forensic reports coming along?"

"We should have them back soon."

When they closed the door, Ettie said, "We have to phone Deirdre's neighbor."

"Let's get ready, call a taxi, and while we're waiting there, you can make that call."

"Okay."

CHAPTER 13

ETTIE DIALED the number of cousin Deirdre's neighbor. She held on for ages and no one answered. She called again and was just about to end the call when the *Englischer* neighbor answered.

"Hello, this is the James' residence."

"Hello, this is Ettie Smith, Deirdre Walton's cousin. I'm wondering if you might do me a favor by giving a message to Deirdre."

"Deirdre's here right now. She's showing me how to make cinnamon cake."

"Oh good. May I speak with her?"

The next thing Ettie heard was the woman bellowing Deirdre's name.

A minute later, a breathless Deirdre came to the phone. "Is that you, Ettie?"

"Jah, it's me."

"I got your letter just today."

"The one about Ebenezer?"

"That's the one. Is that why you're calling?"

"It is."

"The only Ebenezer I can recall is one who passed through here and stayed a couple of weeks. I remember him because there were rumors about him and he was asked to leave."

"Walnut Creek?"

"*Jah.* Not Divine Creek?"

"*Nee.* Here."

"What kind of rumors?"

"He was constantly seen with a woman who wasn't one of us. I don't know all the details. I just heard the rumors, and then he was gone. He had come from somewhere near Divine Creek, they said, and so had the girl."

"How long ago was this?"

"Many years ago. I guess I only remember it because of his unusual name."

"I see, and do you know where he came from or where he went?"

"I only know folks said he came from somewhere close to Divine Creek, but I don't know him from there. I just remember the connection because I used to live there."

"I know. What about any relatives? Did he have any that you know of?"

After a moment, of silence, she said, "I can't recall."

"Think hard. It's important."

"Is that the man who was stabbed? Is that why you're calling?"

"You've heard about him?"

"I heard someone was stabbed. Was that Ebenezer?"

"I'm afraid so. We'd just like to find out more about him. If he has relatives, they should be informed."

88

"I think he had an older brother. Is that helpful?"

"Really?"

"I think so."

"Did you ever meet him?"

"No."

"What makes you think he had one?"

"I don't know. Someone must've mentioned it."

Ettie sighed. *"Denke,* Deirdre. You've been a good help. Can you think really hard and send me a letter by fast mail if you think of anything? Anything at all?"

"I will. I'll give it some good thought, Ettie. How's Elsa-May?"

"She's good. Here's my taxi. I'll have to go."

"Give my love to Elsa-May, would you?"

"I will, and she sends hers."

"Bye, Ettie."

Ettie ended the call.

Elsa-May stepped closer. "Well, what?"

"She thinks he might've had an older *bruder,* but she can't tell me who he was or how she knows that."

"I see. That doesn't help us at all."

Ettie and Elsa-May both climbed into the backseat of the taxi.

AFTER THE SISTERS sat down with Patricia who'd been waiting for them at the café, a waitress came to take their orders. Ettie and Elsa-May decided to share a grilled chicken sandwich with fries, and a pot of hot tea. Patricia only ordered coffee.

When the waitress left, Patricia was the first to speak. "How are you both?"

"Good," Elsa-May said glancing sideways at Ettie.

Feeling her sister's impatience, Ettie wasted no time getting to the heart of the matter. "We found out that one of your patients left you a lot of money."

"That's right he did. The dear old soul. Why does that interest you?" She looked from one sister to the other.

"There would be some that might say that you preyed on the elderly suggesting they leave you money," Elsa-May said.

Ettie hadn't expected Elsa-May to be so brutally honest, but it had to be said.

"Look, I know what you're thinking. Just because someone left me a lot of money everybody's suspicious of me."

"Not just somebody. A patient. A person who was elderly, sick, and possibly easy to manipulate."

"That's why I gave that money to charity, because I didn't want it to ruin my career." Patricia pressed her lips together. "And still, people think ill of me over it."

"What charity did you give it to?" Ettie asked.

Patricia's gaze darted about. "I divided it amongst a few charities. Look, I didn't even know Ebenezer was wealthy. I didn't know this was what you wanted to talk with me about, Ettie."

"Well …"

"I haven't heard anything about being left money and if he did or had intended to do that, he never mentioned anything about it to me. Do you think I killed him for his money? Is that what you think?"

"No," Ettie said.

"That is not the reason I became a nurse and I'm quite upset that you both could think that of me."

"We don't think that of you, but it is a possibility that we thought of. We're just asking a few questions because we thought it was funny that you were there the other day at his house," Elsa-May said.

"I was upset, that's why I was there. I didn't know what else to do. No one else knew him. I couldn't grieve with someone else who knew him. I just wanted to pay my respects and say goodbye in private—have a quiet moment. Can you understand that?"

Elsa-May nodded. "I do. It makes perfect sense to me."

Patricia turned her attention to Ettie. "And what about you, Ettie? Can you understand that?"

"Everybody's different in the way they do things. I hope you don't mind us asking you questions."

The waitress came back and placed their drinks on the table. "The sandwich will be here in a minute or two," she said as she turned around.

"I don't mind at all. If I were in your shoes, I would probably be thinking the very same things."

Elsa-May took a sip of her tea and then placed her cup down on the saucer with a clunk. "Did he mention any friends or anybody he was particularly close with?"

"He mentioned Helga and Levi. Then he mentioned the neighbors, who were always pestering him about one thing after another."

Ettie warmed her hands around her teacup. "Like what?" That sounded different from the information Kelly had given them, that the neighbors had only talked to him once in the whole time they'd lived there.

"He didn't really say and if he did, I probably didn't pay enough attention."

"Was he worried about anything?" Elsa-May asked.

"He didn't say." Patricia brought her coffee cup to her lips, and Ettie noticed the woman was still wearing gloves. The sandwich and fries arrived just then, and they paused long enough to thank the waitress and get plates, napkins, silverware and condiments organized.

"Did Ebenezer ever mention the young man who brought him his food?" asked Ettie as she started in on her half-sandwich.

"No, but he told me he got his food delivered once a week. It was part of my job to check that he got enough food and was capable of preparing it on his own. He had various food allergies and liked his food fresh. Fruit was his favorite."

"We hope you don't mind us asking all these things."

"That's perfectly fine. Although, a little unexpected. I had nothing to do with his death. As a nurse, it's my job to help people. It's ingrained into my nature."

"Did he ever mention a brother?" Elsa-May asked.

"He had a brother?"

"We don't know. Someone thought there might be one."

"He said he was alone in the world. That's what he told me. You might want to look into the Amish man who was there all the time in these last months."

"Gabriel?"

"Yes, that's him."

"And, what about him?" Ettie asked.

"Why did he suddenly show up?"

"Didn't he say?"

"Ebenezer said he wasn't welcome there but he kept coming around, and then Ebenezer just accepted his visits."

Ettie laughed inside. That sure sounded like Gabriel. He was like an over-friendly puppy sometimes.

CHAPTER 14

WHEN THEY FINISHED TALKING to Patricia, they parted on a friendly note. Next on their list was to talk to the fruit boy. Elsa-May and Ettie headed on foot to the markets where he worked, when they saw Ava's buggy approaching. Elsa-May stepped close to the road and waved to her, and she pulled her buggy over to the side.

Ava jumped out to secure her horse. "I've been looking for you two. I went to your *haus*, but you'd already left."

"Are you alone?" Ettie craned her neck looking for Aaron.

"*Jah*. It's *Mamm's* day to look after him today. Have you had the meeting with the nurse?"

"We've only just finished."

"What did you find out?"

"Nothing really. She said a lot of people think that she's preying on old people. She insists she gave the money to various charities."

"I wonder if there's a way to check on that. It's easy

enough for anyone to say they donated the money to charity. Which charities were they?"

Ettie looked at Elsa-May. "She didn't say."

"She was still wearing gloves. Did you notice that Elsa-May?"

"I did. And you'd think she would have taken them off because it wasn't cold in the café."

"Why are you worried about the gloves?"

"Kelly explained to us that it was possible that the killer might've accidentally cut themselves because the knife hit bone and there was something about the angle of the knife handle and such."

"You think she's cut her fingers, so you think she did it?"

"I don't know. We still don't know why anyone had any reason to kill him."

"We were on our way to the markets to find the delivery boy to ask him a few questions. He was at the funeral," Ettie told Ava.

"Jump in and I'll drive you. Let's see if we can find him, shall we?"

The sisters didn't need to be asked twice. Getting a ride was far better than walking.

They drove to the markets and were fortunate enough to see the fruit boy in one corner of the parking lot.

"See him, Elsa-May?"

"Not without my glasses. I need them for close up work, but I can't see very well far away either."

"That's him. He's unloading empty boxes from that pickup truck."

"I'll park here further away if you want to speak to him, Ettie."

"Denke, Ava."

"I'll go with you," Elsa-May said.

THE ELDERLY SISTERS walked over to him, and he looked up when they were close.

"Excuse me. Do you think we might have a word with you?"

"You're Ebenezer's friends?"

"Yes, we are. I met you at the funeral," Ettie said. "You're Pete, right?" When he nodded and kept the same vague expression, Ettie figured he was probably thinking that most Amish people looked the same.

"What's this about?" he asked.

"We just want to ask you about Ebenezer. It won't take long."

"Sure." He dropped the box he was carrying. "What do you want to know?"

"We know that you and he spent a bit of time together."

"That's true. We always talked after I delivered his food. He was always my last job of the day so I wouldn't have to hurry."

"Was he worried about anything in particular recently?"

"He said someone wanted him to get off his land. He was worried he might not be able to stay. I said he could stay with me until he found somewhere else."

"But wasn't he the owner of the land?"

"I don't think so."

"And he didn't want to leave?"

"That's right."

"Who wanted him to leave?"

"It was a woman, I think." He folded his arms across his chest and it was then that Ettie noticed his hands had cuts on them.

"What about Ebenezer's neighbors? You were talking with them at the funeral."

"What about them?"

"Do you know them?"

"I'd never met them before the funeral. I guess you could say I know them now. What's this all about?"

"We're trying to work out who killed him."

"I talked to the police already. I don't have anything more to say."

"We're just—"

"Look, I don't know who you think you are, but this conversation is over." He turned away from them, and Ettie stepped forward to ask another question but Elsa-May gripped her arm.

"Let's go Ettie." Elsa-May slowly turned her sister around by her shoulders.

When they got back inside Ava's buggy, Ava asked, "I was watching everything from here. He didn't look too happy at the end. What did you find out?"

"Nothing really. He got upset about something. Did you see his hands, Elsa-May?"

"*Nee.*"

"They were red and cut."

"Really?"

"*Jah.*"

"That might just be from the kind of work he does. He'd be scraping his hands on the wooden fruit boxes. What do you think, Ava?"

"It's hard to say, but I think that might be right."

Ettie sighed. "Can you drive us back to Ebenezer's *haus*, Ava?"

"What do you hope to find there?"

"I want to talk to the neighbors."

"Sure. What are you going to ask them?" Ava checked in her rearview mirror and then clicked her horse forward.

"I'll think of something before I get there. I need to know why Pete the fruit boy got upset when I mentioned them."

"Let's go."

CHAPTER 15

AVA STAYED IN THE BUGGY, while Ettie and Elsa-May walked up to the neighbors' house and knocked on the door.

Ettie's heart thumped hard. She didn't like talking to people she didn't know, and it was worse when she had to ask questions.

Jack Simpson opened the door and stared at both of them. "Hello, again." His words were hesitant.

"Hello. I'm wondering if you might be able to answer some questions."

"About Ebenezer from next door," Elsa-May added.

"What kind of questions?" He eyed them carefully. "What's this about? I hardly knew the man."

"Did he own the house next door or was he leasing it?"

"If you're trying to find the owner, I can't help you. We only talked once and that was when the fence fell down and he wouldn't do a thing about fixing it. As far as I know he was the owner, but I never knew a thing about him."

Ettie noticed his hand when he put it behind his back. "You hurt your hand?"

He pulled it out from behind his back and Ettie noted it was his right hand. "Yes."

"How did you do that?" Elsa-May asked.

"Horse bite."

"Really?" Elsa-May asked. "When did the horse bite you?"

At once, Ettie knew Elsa-May had gone too far.

"Look, it's none of your business. Why you are asking me all these ridiculous questions?"

"We're trying to find out who killed Ebenezer."

"Isn't that a job for the police?"

"Yes."

He frowned. "I've got better things to do with my time." The man stepped back inside and slammed the door.

Elsa-May looked over at Ettie. "That went well. You're not losing your touch."

Ettie sighed. "True, and neither are you, I'd say."

They were getting nowhere and not only that, they were alienating the very people who might have valuable information.

Suddenly the door swung open and the man pointed to the road. "Get off my property."

"We're going." Ettie and Elsa-May hurried down the porch steps and continued to the buggy waiting at the bottom of the long driveway.

"Looked like he was angry," Ava said when they got back into the buggy.

"His hand was bandaged and he got upset when we asked him about it," Elsa-May said.

Ava wasted no time turning the buggy around.

"He said a horse bit his hand."

"Thanks for driving us around today, Ava, but I think we need to go home now and put up our feet and have a rest."

Ava giggled. *"Denke* for letting me come with you."

"We couldn't have covered so much ground today if it wasn't for you, so we're the ones thanking you," Elsa-May said.

Ettie remembered their original plan for the day. "Elsa-May, we planned to go to Helga's place and ask her why she lied about things."

Elsa-May shook her head. "Not today. I can't face asking any more questions. We'll do it tomorrow."

CHAPTER 16

ON FRIDAY MORNING, Ettie sat with Elsa-May at the kitchen table nibbling on toast spread with honey. All night she hadn't been able to sleep because she was thinking about Ebenezer's neighbors. Now it was morning, and she was bothered again by the nurse and not looking forward to facing Helga.

"What are you thinking about, Ettie? I can see the gears of your mind slowly turning like the cogs on a wheel."

Ettie clicked her tongue. "I think we should go back to Ebenezer's *haus*."

"What for?"

"Because I think we should have a look at whatever's there."

"A clue or something?"

"Hopefully, a clue. We might find what the nurse was looking for that day she came when we were there. The morning after Ebenezer was found."

"Maybe she went back and found it, whatever it was."

"Anything's possible." Ettie shrugged. "Ebenezer, a man who had no apparent history shows up in the community lying about where he was from. He must've been hiding amongst us, but from what? The question is, was he ever one of us at all?"

Elsa-May's eyes popped open. "Now that's a thought."

"He wasn't a member of Divine Creek according to the original bishop, so maybe everything he said about himself was a lie.".

"Was Ebenezer Fuller even his real name?" Elsa-May asked.

"Kelly would hopefully find that out, if possible. I'll feel better if I can go back to his *haus* and take another look around. Undisturbed by visitors, this time."

"Okay. At least it doesn't look like we're going to get caught in a blizzard yet today."

"Doesn't it?" Ettie asked looking at the gray sky.

"Nee."

"So you've had a good look outside, have you?"

"I can see it from here. I don't need to sit staring out the window like you do."

"Speaking of looking out the window, I wonder if the place next door will sit there empty forever."

"It's going to be hard to sell."

"It's a shame. It's a nice house."

"And it's got good neighbors."

Both sisters chuckled.

"We could even bake them a pie every now and again," Elsa-May said.

"I'd be happy to do that if anyone ever moves in."

Elsa-May nodded to Ettie's half-eaten toast. "Finish your breakfast and then we can start our day."

"Okay."

Elsa-May hung on to the table and stood up. "I feel bad leaving Snowy again today. He much prefers having us stay home."

"He sleeps all day. He won't even notice we're gone."

"Do you really think we should go to Ebenezer's?"

"I do."

Elsa-May sighed. "All right. I'll go with you, but only to keep you out of trouble."

WHEN THEY GOT to Ebenezer's house, Ettie pushed open the creaky door, walked in, and sniffed the air. "It's musty in here."

Elsa-May moved in behind her and closed the door. "It's been closed up for days. Do you really think we'll find something the police missed?"

"*Jah,* I do. Maybe they didn't know what they were looking for."

"Well, what are *we* looking for?"

Ettie looked around the living room. "I don't know yet. You start poking around in the kitchen and I'll go through the cupboards in here and try to find some personal papers."

Elsa-May headed to the kitchen while Ettie opened the cupboard that was built into the wall of the living room. Seeing a stack of Amish newspapers, she lowered herself onto the floor and pulled them out.

Coming out of the kitchen, Elsa-May said, "There's nothing in there. Just a few pots and pans."

"Look in the bedrooms."

SAMANTHA PRICE

When Elsa-May left the room, Ettie noticed there were some letters in between two of the papers. She took hold of them, and got up from the hard floorboards and headed over to the couch to read them. Ettie was disappointed when she saw the letters weren't addressed to Ebenezer. "Elsa-May, I just found a couple of letters."

Elsa-May came hurrying toward her and sat down with her. "What do they say?"

"They're not his. They're for the people next door. They must have been mistakenly delivered to him and he never passed them along."

"That's dreadful."

"What that's telling me is that he didn't like them."

Ettie placed the letters on the couch beside her. "Let's keep looking."

Elsa-May went back to the bedroom and just as Ettie was back to fishing through the newspapers hoping to find something else, she looked up and noticed there was a top shelf within the cupboard. She stood up and that's when she noticed a white box pushed back on the shelf. Standing on her tiptoes and stretching up, she still couldn't reach it.

Looking around, she saw nothing to stand on, so she carried a chair from the kitchen. Nervously, she stood on it hoping it wouldn't topple, and then she put both hands on the box. It was light—it almost felt like there was nothing in it. Now she couldn't get down and hold the box at the same time. "Elsa-May, help me."

Elsa-May came out of the bedroom. "Careful!"

"Take the box from me so I can get down."

Elsa-May did so, and when Ettie was safely on the floor, she took the box from Elsa-May and headed to the couch. Slowly, she opened the box to see one solitary piece of paper. With Elsa-May still watching, Ettie picked it up and unfolded it.

"What is it this time? More inaccurately addressed letters?"

"No, look at this." She handed the note to Elsa-May, who read it out.

"I'm sorry I can't do this anymore. Meet you at the boundary, and this has to be sorted once and for all." Elsa-May looked at Ettie in shock. "This looks like … exactly like the letter Kelly found. Also, it's got the same squiggle for a signature."

"Exactly the same, but different. The same person wrote it about the same kind of thing."

"I know and they both mention boundaries and if I'm not wrong they're both in the same handwriting."

Ettie narrowed her eyes at her sister. "I just said that."

"Me too. Why didn't Kelly's people find it, though?"

"They probably didn't know what they were looking for."

Elsa-May nodded. "You might be right. They would've been looking for fingerprints, blood spatter patterns and more murder weapons." They both looked at each other when they heard a car. "Uh-oh. This can't be good."

"Nee!"

"What should we do?"

Elsa-May pulled the curtains aside, and groaned, "It's Kelly."

CHAPTER 17

"If only it was anybody but Kelly." Ettie bit her lip knowing he was going to be upset with them. "Do you think we should hide?"

"*Nee.* He'd find us and then we'd look foolish."

"What will we say? He'll want to know why we're here."

Elsa-May flung her hands into the air. "We'll just tell the truth."

Ettie was amazed Elsa-May was calm, and pleased that her sister was walking to the door. Better that he saw her sister first. "The truth? Good idea! I know he's going to look at us in disappointment, though."

"*Jah,* but that will turn into joy when he sees what we've found."

"We've both just put our fingerprints all over it. That will cancel everything out." When Elsa-May hesitated at the door, Ettie urged her on, "Open the door for him."

"You first."

Ettie said a quick prayer that Kelly wouldn't be mad,

made sure Elsa-May was right behind her, and then flung open the front door.

He didn't look mad. He stepped back in shock staring at Ettie and then noticing Elsa-May. "What the devil are you two doing here?"

"She made me come," Elsa-May said pointing at Ettie.

Ettie turned around and stared at her sister in shock.

Kelly placed his hands on his hips. "You can't just come into someone's house and start nosing around. This is wrong."

"We thought it was all right since the police tape is down."

"Yes, and we found something very interesting," Elsa-May said.

"Is that right?"

They both nodded furiously.

"Come inside out of the cold," Ettie said, even though it was nearly as cold within the house.

He walked past them and when they closed the door, he turned around to face them. "What was it you found?"

"Where is it, Ettie?"

"I gave it to you."

"You didn't! You had it when you were on the chair."

Kelly clamped his lips together in disapproval. "Mrs. Smith, you were on a chair?"

Ettie was so annoyed with Elsa-May losing the valuable evidence that she ignored Kelly completely. "I handed it to you so I could get down."

"No, you handed me the box, Ettie."

Kelly raised his hands in the air. "Stop! Tell me what it was and I'll help you find it. If you just had it, whatever it was, it can't have gone far. What was it?"

"It was a note talking about boundaries and in the same handwriting as the note you showed us at the station. The one you found in the kitchen after Ebenezer died."

His eyebrows flew up. "Retrace your steps."

They all went into the living room, and Elsa-May squealed, "Here it is!" She reached down to the floor and picked it up. It had fallen between two couches.

He glared at the note. "What are you doing, Mrs. Lutz?" He pulled a pair of tweezers and a plastic bag out of his pocket. Carefully, he took the note from Elsa-May's fingers with the tweezer ends and popped it into the plastic bag before he held it up to the light to read it. "I think you're right. I think this is from the same person who wrote the letter we have in evidence." He looked across at Ettie. "Where in the world did you find it?"

"Just in that cupboard."

"Inside one of the newspapers?"

"No. It was in a box in the cupboard. It was white and the base of the box was white, so it is possible your team thought it was just an empty box."

"I find it hard to believe they missed something like that. I'll get them to come back and give the place a more thorough going over in case they've missed something else."

"Glad to be of help," Elsa-May said.

He frowned at her. "I could have you both charged, do you know that?"

Ettie gulped.

Kelly continued, "Tampering with evidence, trespassing, obstruction of justice, and that's just off the top of my head."

Elsa-May grimaced. "We're helping."

"That still doesn't make it right that you're here. I've got many people who help me, and they don't contaminate evidence."

"We didn't know it was evidence until we saw what it said. We're just trying to find out who Ebenezer was." Ettie said. "We were only looking for a clue to his identity. He might've been using a false name. We really don't know who he was."

"There are other ways for you to find that out. Talk to everyone like you normally do."

Elsa-May asked, "Did you find out anything about him that you're not telling us? It'll save us time if you'd let us know."

"We didn't come up with a match for his prints in our system."

"I suppose that's a good thing," Elsa-May said smiling.

"His dental records don't match any missing persons either."

"Did you find out anything that was useful?" Ettie asked him.

"I suppose it won't hurt to tell you. It's possible there might be more than one perpetrator."

Elsa-May gasped. "Two people stabbed him?"

"That's what it's looking like so far. The lab informed me there are three different blood samples. Two on the victim and a third from here in the house. Keep that to yourselves."

"Of course. We won't tell anybody."

"I didn't think you would."

Ettie stepped closer to him. "Anything else you can tell us?"

"I can tell you we're following up on a lead. Now, I better get this to the fingerprint team." He looked down at the plastic covered note.

"What is the lead?" Ettie asked.

"I can't tell you just yet. It won't make a difference to what you're doing."

"Can't you tell us? It might help us to help you better."

Kelly sighed. "Keep this to yourselves. Ebenezer didn't own this place and we're tracking down the owner." He judged their reactions to the news. "Please tell me you weren't aware of that."

Elsa-May said, "Everyone thought it was his. He's lived here for years and years. Since he arrived here."

A smile hinted around Kelly's lips, the way it did when he knew he was onto something. That made Ettie wonder if Kelly knew a lot more about everything than he was letting on.

"Have you talked with Ebenezer's nurse again?"

Kelly narrowed his eyes at Ettie. "Yes, why? Do you know something about her that I don't? You're always talking about her."

"She just seems odd to me."

Kelly stepped forward. "In what way, and what do you know about her?"

"Just tell him, Ettie and get it over with."

Ettie frowned not wanting to tell Kelly that they'd been there in the house with the nurse that first day after Ebenezer was killed. "Helga didn't ever see her here. So, how do we know she was?"

Kelly shook his head. "She only visited every few weeks."

"We know for a fact that she came to this very house and disregarded the crime-tape all around it."

His eyes bore through Ettie's. "Who told you that?"

"No one told us. We saw her with our very own eyes."

"All right!" Elsa-May spoke so loud that it made Ettie jump. "I'll admit it. We came through the crime tape."

Kelly's eyes blazed with fury. "You what? That's twice you've done a dreadful thing." He shook his head. "I'm very disappointed in the both of you. I've put my trust in you and you've thrown it back in my face."

Ettie stared at Elsa-May hoping she'd say something to help them get back into Kelly's good graces. Instead, Elsa-May said, "I didn't want to do it. Ettie talked me into it."

Ettie's mind went blank and her tongue started flapping. "Only because I knew your evidence collecting people had been and gone. We figured they'd made an error and forgotten to take the tape away. While we were inside, she comes in as bold as day and walks right on into the house. That's what you should be troubled about, Detective Kelly. You know we didn't kill him, but she very well might've."

"That's right," Elsa-May agreed. "She didn't even say why she was here. Had she come to remove evidence that she'd left behind? Hmm?"

Kelly sighed. "Tell me everything from start to finish. From the time you entered the house, when she came in and when she left."

Ettie told Kelly everything, then added, "I didn't think she was a nurse at all. She wears too much make-up, but she must be because when she drove us to town, she drove into the parking area of the doctors' offices, and when we walked away, she walked inside."

"I know she's a nurse. I'll look into it. I have questioned her, and you're right, she doesn't look like a nurse, but she is. You both need to promise me that you'll respect the law." He dipped his head and looked at them from under his bushy eyebrows.

"We do and we will," Ettie said.

"That goes for me too," Elsa-May said.

"I'll drive you ladies home."

It wasn't a question, it was an order and with the mood he was in, Ettie and Elsa-May weren't about to argue with him.

CHAPTER 18

THAT EVENING, Ettie and Elsa-May were talking while cooking the evening meal. The subject of their conversations was still who might've killed Ebenezer.

"Who owned the land, Elsa-May? I wish there was some way we could find out."

"We'll find out in time."

"I would rather know now. I'm switching from the nurse to the neighbors. He had his hand bandaged and I'm not sure if I believe his story."

"If he did it, then why?"

Ettie looked over at Elsa-May. "Do you have to ask me that after what happened here?"

"Oh, that's right." Elsa-May chuckled. "It's always the neighbors?"

Smiling, Ettie said, "I suppose it's not the neighbors in every case, though. We just happened to have odd ones."

"Kelly always said that it's people closest to the victim who are the likely suspects."

Elsa-May chuckled. "He didn't mean closest to the victim in proximity he meant —"

"I know what he meant. And since Ebenezer didn't have a family, maybe he was closest with the neighbors, and they're choosing to deny it. What about that?"

"They flatly deny they were close and Gabriel didn't make mention of them. They said they only talked with him once in all those years."

"Well, they would say that if they'd killed him, wouldn't they? If they were guilty, they wouldn't want people to know how well they knew him."

"Helga said she hardly saw anyone at his place. I knew we should've gone back to talk to her and we would've if Kelly hadn't come to the house yesterday."

"Maybe Helga never saw the neighbors at his *haus* because they were inside the place when she drove her buggy past. Then their vehicles wouldn't be seen from outside because they would've walked there."

"True but, neither did she mention the nurse, or Gabriel, or the fruit boy. He acted weirdly too."

"Maybe we frightened him, Ettie. Anyway, let's sit down to eat this meal we've been blessed with and we'll put it out of our minds while we're at the table."

Ettie pulled out the chair. "Sounds like a good idea to me." She looked down at the leftovers from the night before—meatloaf, and the vegetables they'd cooked to go with it.

As soon as they were both seated and about to give thanks, a loud knock sounded on their door.

"Botheration!" What Elsa-May disliked most was being interrupted at mealtimes. "I'll put our plates in the oven."

Before Ettie got to the door, a voice rang out, "Yoo hoo! Is anyone home?"

Ettie opened the door to see a flustered-looking Ruth Esh wringing her hands.

"Ruth, what's the matter?"

Elsa-May stood behind Ettie. "Come inside," Elsa-May insisted.

Ruth hurried through the doorway and Ettie closed the door behind her. Ruth took a deep breath, and then she leaned against the wall.

"What is it that's got you so upset, Ruth?" Elsa-May asked.

"He was married!"

BOTH ETTIE and Elsa-May knew who Ruth was talking about.

"Give me your coat and then sit down, Ruth."

Once Elsa-May had Ruth's coat, Ettie led their visitor into the living room. "How did you find out he was married?"

Ruth flopped onto the couch. "No one ever knew about it. She wasn't even mentioned at the funeral. I called a friend of mine in Walker County and sure enough she remembers a man called Ebenezer and he was married."

"How do we know if it was the same Ebenezer? We heard he came from a place close to Divine Creek. Oh wait, is Walker County close to Divine Creek?"

"It's not far. Divine Creek is just outside the county line. My friend told me he wasn't married very long, and why he didn't bring her back to his community—because he left for her. That's where he's from, Walker County! I reached out to all my friends. I wrote to every community I could, asking about Ebenezer. I knew someone would have to know him. You see, the woman he married was an outsider—an *Englischer*. It caused a fuss when he left the community for her."

"Of course it would," Ettie said.

"*Ach,* that is a little odd," Elsa-May said. "Now he's back. What happened to the marriage? Did she die?"

"No wonder we knew nothing about her if she wasn't one of us," Ettie said. "I don't know how he could keep something like that to himself."

"It seems Ebenezer was good at keeping secrets." Ruth put her hands on her cheeks. "I should've insisted I get proper records when he first came here. It's all my fault."

Ettie patted her on the back. "You weren't to know. You can't blame yourself for something like that."

"If I can't blame myself, who can I blame?"

"Well, no one," Ettie said.

"Sometimes these things just aren't anybody's fault. He didn't want anybody to know where he was from or that he was married to an *Englischer*."

"Did she die?" Elsa-May asked once more.

"I don't know. We'll have to try to find her and let her know he died."

"Did they divorce, or what?" Ettie asked.

"I don't know the answer to all these questions. I've got people looking into it."

"What kind of people?"

"My friends from the other communities."

Ettie flung her hand in the air. "That's it! That's why he had a beard. He was married."

Elsa-May raised her eyebrows. "That's right. I never gave it a second thought."

"Her name was Elaine," Ruth stated.

"You know her name?" Ettie asked, stunned.

"*Jah.* Elaine, last name Greene. Greene, with an e on the end. My friend particularly remembered that. Elaine's father was a farmer, and a wealthy one. The family were well known around the district."

"Why didn't you tell us you knew her name right away, Ruth?"

"So her name was Elaine—"

"Greene," Elsa-May finished Ettie's sentence. "What else do you know about her?"

Ruth shrugged her shoulders. "They were only married for a couple of weeks when they separated. The rest, I can't tell you. My friend said she heard that they fought like cat and dog, and not friendly cats and dogs. I have a cat and a dog and they get along, but that's because they grew up together."

"How does your friend know for sure this is the same Ebenezer?"

"There aren't too many with that name and what's more, his *bruder* wound up in Divine Creek for a while. That's more than a coincidence. That's how he knew about Divine Creek. The time frame of the marriage all fits in with him leaving there to when he arrived here."

"So Deirdre was right," said Ettie excitedly. "There is a *bruder*."

"Yes, but I don't know anything much about him," said Ruth as she sniffed the air. "What's that lovely smell. Pot roast?"

"*Jah.* Well, meatloaf and vegetables. Stay and join us,"

Elsa-May said. "We were just about to sit down and there's plenty."

"I've already eaten. It's fine. I won't keep you from your delicious smelling dinner. I just thought you should know that he was married. I was so shocked when I found out and I knew you would be too."

"Do you have any idea at all where Elaine is now?"

"*Nee*, but I'll find her. She should know about Ebenezer."

"Why did the bishop think he was unmarried?"

"That's something you'd have to ask him," Ruth said. "He might've known, but not been at liberty to say anything."

Ettie nodded.

Ruth jumped to her feet. "I'll find out what I can and I'll let you know the second I find out anything more."

"*Denke*, Ruth." They showed her to the door.

Once Ruth's buggy was rattling down the road, Elsa-May closed the door. "What do you think about that, Ettie?"

"Well, I think that it's a shock. It will be a shock to everybody."

"Solves the mystery of why he never married. He already was married."

Ettie sat back down at the kitchen table, and Elsa-May got their food out of the oven, and placed the plates down on the table.

After they said their silent prayer of thanks for the food, Ettie opened her eyes and picked up her fork. When she noticed Elsa-May hadn't moved, she looked over and saw her staring into space. "You're not getting sick or something, are you?" Ettie popped a forkful of meatloaf into her mouth.

"Just thinking and wondering about Ebenezer hiding he was married." She looked down at her food. "Hopefully, we'll be able to eat this without further interruptions."

Ettie swallowed. "I hope so. It's delicious. We'll have to tell Kelly about Ebenezer's wife. He doesn't know." Ettie dropped her fork. "She killed him, Elsa-May!"

"Why do you say that?"

"Remember that Kelly once told us that they're most suspicious of the spouses first?"

Elsa-May finished her mouthful.

"What I can't figure out is why Detective Kelly didn't find this information out for himself."

"You said that already, Ettie. Let's stop by to see him tomorrow and ask him, shall we?"

"Of course."

Elsa-May nodded. "We'll have to tell him what we know."

"We'll go first thing tomorrow. Now we've got her name, he should be able to get access to records. Elaine Greene was her maiden name. I wonder if she's still alive."

"If she's not, she wouldn't have killed him."

Ettie frowned at her sister's comment, and then popped another forkful of food into her mouth. Then she realized what Elsa-May had said, and started giggling. It wasn't long before her sister joined in.

CHAPTER 19

BEFORE THEY LEFT the next morning, they got a visit from Ava, who'd come without her baby again. They sat Ava down and told her their latest news.

"Have you told Kelly yet?" Ava asked.

"We're doing that today."

"*Jah*, we're on our way to tell him."

"I'll take you there," Ava said.

"That's not necessary. We can call him from the phone down the road."

"I have a free day. I can take you wherever you need to go."

"We could do with getting some things from the markets, Ettie. We can do that after we talk with Kelly."

"What do we need?"

"We're running out of flour."

Ettie sighed. "We're forever running out of things. Didn't we just shop a week ago?"

"*Jah*, Ettie, but we have to eat three times a day, remember?"

"I suppose so."

"Well? Am I driving you? You should take advantage of my offer. I'm only without Aaron for two days a week."

Ettie smiled, glad to save a taxi fare and enjoy Ava's company. "Very well. *Denke* for the kind offer, Ava."

Ava sat in the buggy while Ettie and Elsa-May walked into the station. Just when Ettie was asking the officer behind the desk if they could see Detective Kelly for a moment, Kelly walked out from the back area looking flustered.

He hurried over to them. "You're here to see me?"

"Yes."

"You'll have to be quick. I'm on my way out. We just learned he was married. Couldn't you have found that out? Wouldn't you have known?"

"That's what we came here to tell you."

"We only found out last night," Ettie said.

"With all your access to records, why didn't you find it out sooner?"

He pressed his lips together and glared at Elsa-May. "Because, Mrs. Lutz, he wasn't Ebenezer Fuller. He was Ebenezer Swarey."

Ettie moved in front of Elsa-May. "What?"

"Ebenezer Swarey."

"Is his wife still alive?"

"Yes, very much alive and I'm heading to her right now to arrest her."

Ettie gasped, and under her breath, she said, "I was right."

"Still, it would've been helpful to know this sooner, but our hard efforts have paid off and any minute now I'll be on my way to arrest Elaine Wicks. That's the name she goes by these days. She has been using her mother's maiden name, we found out."

"How can you be sure she's the murderer?" Elsa-May asked.

"Detective work and following leads pays off. She lives out of town. We happen to know she has been here for a week staying at the Deer Acres Guest House. On the day he was murdered, she was treated for cuts on her hands at one of the local hospitals. And you remember what I told you about the attacker and the knife?"

Elsa-May winced.

"Did she confess to the crime?" Ettie asked.

"No! But putting the pieces together, she's guilty."

"What pieces?"

He rolled his eyes and repeated, "She lives hundreds of miles north of here, and she happened to be here on the day he died and we know that because we have hospital records from the emergency department. I spoke to the doctor who treated her and the injury was consistent with her stabbing someone. You see, more often than not, in knife attacks the perpetrator often injures his own hand."

"Yes. You mentioned that the other day, Detective. No need to tell us again."

Kelly grinned, and told them over again, "On the knife, there wasn't a good enough handle for her to get a good enough grip. When she stabbed into the victim's bone, the knife would have stopped. Her hand kept going, and she cut herself in the process. She had three cuts on her fingers and he was stabbed five times. We need a blood match and we're done. Case closed. We'll also match her handwriting to the notes we found."

"Are you certain it's she?"

"Very. I obtained those records from the hospital and talked to the coroner. After examining the records, the knife and the victim, it was the coroner's opinion the injuries on her hand were consistent with her being the attacker."

Elsa-May shook her head. "We get the picture. So, you're going to arrest this woman for certain?"

"We're obtaining a warrant as we speak and once it comes through I'm taking a long drive to make the arrest." His phone beeped and he pulled it out of his pocket, spoke with someone briefly, then ended the call and popped it back into his pocket. "Okay, Conrad's got the warrant in his hand and he's waiting for me out front. I'm on my way." He nodded to them and then he was gone.

"Elsa-May, didn't he say there were three lots of blood?"

"He did."

"I hope he's not going to arrest the wrong person. And, he's arresting her before he knows if her blood matches the samples he's got. Isn't he?"

"Sounds like it. What will we do now, Ettie? Go home?"

"*Nee!* Something's not right. Let's finally go see what Helga has to say. We're long overdue to find out why she's been keeping things from us. If she's been keeping things from us, she's been keeping things from the police."

"Helga?"

"*Jah.* I don't think she's told us the truth."

"What about our shopping, and the flour?"

"We'll do that later. We should've gone to see Helga days ago." Ettie walked out of the station and Elsa-May followed.

CHAPTER 20

ON THE WAY to Helga's, Elsa-May said to Ava, "We do appreciate you going out of your way for us like this."

"I need a break in my routine sometimes."

"How can he say for certain the wife did it before he even talks with her?" Ettie asked.

Ava said, "He's got enough to make an arrest, and he hopes that while he's holding her they'll do DNA testing."

"No one knew about his wife you see, Ava, because he moved communities, lied about where he was from and used a different last name."

"Ettie, tell me again why we're going to Helga's? Why do you think she lied?"

"Think back, Elsa-May. The nurse regularly visited, the fruit man visited, and Helga never mentioned those people. Or Gabriel. She said there was never anyone there."

"That's true. We'll see what she has to say about it."

Ettie rolled her eyes. "Good idea."

. . .

JUST AS THEY had driven past Ebenezer's house, they saw the fruit boy coming out of the neighbors' house. "Look at that! They're talking and laughing as friendly as can be."

"I see that."

"Pete Ross said he just met the Simpsons at the funeral. They look like they're old friends, if you ask me."

Ava agreed, "He's a young boy and they're an older couple. What could they possibly have in common?"

"Perhaps, killing Ebenezer?"

"Why though, Ettie?"

"I don't know, but something's not right here. I've got to call Kelly and tell him not to arrest that poor woman."

"Why? She could be the killer, Ettie."

"I'll call him from Helga's phone in her barn and let him know what we just saw."

"He won't listen to you," Elsa-May said. "Besides, do you have his cell phone number?"

Ettie tapped the side of her head. "It's in here."

When they got to Helga's house, they were greeted by her and Ettie told her she had an urgent call to make. While the others went in the house with Helga, Ettie headed to the barn.

After she blew off a layer of dust, she picked up the phone's receiver and dialed the number she knew by heart.

He answered in his usual bored tone. "Detective Kelly."

"Detective Kelly, it's Ettie Smith here."

"Mrs. Smith, didn't I just see you at the station?"

"Yes, but there's something urgent you should know about."

"What's that?"

"Elsa-May, Ava, and I were driving to Helga's house

and just as well because we just drove past Ebenezer's house and we saw Ebenezer's fruit boy talking to the people who live in between Helga and Ebenezer."

"And?"

"And they looked guilty when we saw them. The fruit boy hurried to his truck. They were laughing about something when the boy was walking out of the house with Jack."

"What are you saying and why's that important? You think they've conspired together to kill Ebenezer?"

"Not necessarily, but don't you think you need to look into things like this before arresting Elaine Greene?"

"Mrs. Smith, firstly, it's not Elaine Greene, it's Elaine Wicks. You know the pressure I'm under. This case has to be closed as quick as possible. I don't have time to chase shadows."

"I know, but—"

"We have evidence she's guilty, Mrs. Smith, and we have more coming."

"I didn't tell you before because I thought you'd think I was stupid, but the neighbor has his hand bandaged and he said it was a horse bite. What if—?

"Mrs. Smith, he already told us he cut his hand on the knife by accident when he discovered the body."

"But—"

"Trust me on this. I have to go. Goodbye."

The call ended with a click. Ettie moved the receiver away from her ear and stared at it. "How rude." Ettie replaced the receiver and made her way back to Helga's house, upset that Kelly had dismissed what they'd seen.

When Ettie walked into the living room, Elsa-May looked up. "What did he say?"

Ettie shook her head as she slumped onto the couch between Helga and Ava. "He didn't listen."

"What did you have to tell the detective that was so urgent?" Helga asked.

Ettie wasn't prepared to tell her and hoped the others hadn't. "You've been keeping something from us, Helga!"

Helga stared wide-eyed at Ettie. "What are you talking about?"

"You didn't tell us that Ebenezer and Levi were brothers."

CHAPTER 21

"WHAT ARE YOU SAYING, ETTIE?" Elsa-May asked, her eyebrows all but disappearing beneath her prayer *kapp*.

"It's true." Helga sighed and clasped her hands in her lap in a vain attempt to stop their obvious shaking. "We were sure no one would ever find out. Ebenezer and Levi both thought it best. They were never close and—"

"Wait! What's this about?" Elsa-May asked.

"Ebenezer and Levi were brothers, Elsa-May. They both had the same last name of Swarey."

"How do you know, Ettie?"

"I worked it out. I remembered that Levi came from around that same vicinity where we found out Ebenezer was from. Also, they looked quite similar. They had the same shaped ears. You can tell a lot by a person's ears. Ebenezer wasn't the only one who changed his last name was he, Helga?"

"You're right, Ettie. When I first met Levi, he was Levi Swarey and then when he decided to start courting me he changed his name to Smucker and moved here before we married. He didn't want it known he was Ebenezer's *bruder*. Then the worst thing happened. Ebenezer moved close to us. He'd married that dreadful woman and brought shame to the Swarey family. To get away from everything, he moved away and changed his name. That's why he lived as a recluse the way he did."

Elsa-May said. "That aside, you told us no one was ever at Ebenezer's place and now we know that to be a lie."

Helga breathed out heavily and then put her hand to her forehead. "The trouble is, when you tell one lie you have to cover it with another." Helga licked her lips. "When I said no one, I meant hardly anyone was there. Sometimes there were people. I just didn't want to be questioned about them. I don't want to get involved in all this. It'll be too hard on Levi. He still hasn't recovered from seeing our neighbor bending over his brother's life-less body."

Ettie folded her arms across her chest. "Don't want to be questioned about them? Who is 'them'?"

"There were a number of people there from time to time."

"How often was the nurse there?" asked Elsa-May.

Helga stared across the room.

Ettie asked, "What is it about the nurse? Do you think that the nurse killed him, Helga?"

"*Ach nee.* I wouldn't think that—is that what *you* think, Ettie?"

"I notice she wears gloves even when she's inside. Kelly told us the murderer most likely has cuts on their hands, did you know that? Maybe she's covering her wounds."

"*Nee*, Ettie. She has a cut on her hand because she was here having tea, she dropped it and then cut her hand. It was a small cut. Nothing at all."

"She was here, in this *haus?*"

Helga sighed. "That's right. She was here and cut her hand on the broken glass."

"Glass?" Elsa-May asked. "Glass or a cup? You said tea, and then you said glass. You don't drink hot tea from a glass. No one I know does that, anyway. I've never seen it done."

"Errr …. A glass. She asked for a glass of water."

"Was that on the day he died?" Ava asked.

"It could've been."

"Think hard, Helga!" Elsa-May leaned forward.

Ettie said, "Maybe she came here after he died. Maybe she was covering her tracks. Covering up the truth and giving herself an alibi and a convenient excuse for her cut."

"Oh, Ettie, you cannot think that." Helga frowned.

"Was she wearing gloves when she arrived?"

Helga was silent for a moment and crossed one leg over the other under her full dress. "I can't remember if she was or not."

"Did you see the cut?"

"*Nee*. She left right away saying she had a first aid kit in the car. I looked out the window a few minutes later and she was gone."

"What I want to know is why was she here? Are you two friends?" Elsa-May asked. "Why was she having tea, or water, or whatever, here in the first instance?"

"I barely know her. I've done nothing wrong. Why are you asking these things?"

Elsa-May said, "You have done wrong, Helga. You lied by covering up the fact that Ebenezer was your *bruder*-in-law."

Her mouth turned down at the corners. "I had nothing to do with his death."

"No one thinks you did, but were you friends with Patricia?"

"Just tell us the truth," Ava said, in her soft and kind voice.

Helga stared at Ava. "I wasn't going to mention it because I do have a few English friends and I know that's not acceptable to some people."

"How close a friend was she?" Ava asked.

"She'd come over here after she had been to see Ebenezer. We'd have a cup of tea and talk. She'd keep me informed how he was getting along. I did care about him."

Ettie was pleased that finally they were hearing the truth. "What kind of person did she seem like to you?"

"Very kind. She was very caring and concerned about Ebenezer."

"I think we should go, Ettie. Ava probably needs to get home."

"*Jah*, I do."

Helga moved in her seat. "You're welcome to stay for a bite to eat. Levi should be home soon, but I can give you something to eat first if you're in a hurry."

"That's quite all right. We have somewhere else to be, and Ava needs to pick up her son." Ettie smiled at Helga hoping they hadn't upset her too much.

. . .

As Ava's buggy traveled away from Helga's house, Ava said, "Why would the nurse befriend Helga?"

"I don't know. I don't think we've gotten to the bottom of it. I'm shocked that Helga didn't tell us her husband and Ebenezer were kinfolk. Levi let Ebenezer go to his grave without admitting to anyone that they were closely related. Not even the bishop knew."

"It's unbelievable," Elsa-May said.

"Also, when I called Kelly, he told me that the neighbor cut his hand on the murder weapon when he found the body. That's what the man's claiming. It wasn't a horse bite like he told us."

Elsa-May shook her head. "So many lies."

Ava nodded. *"Jah*, but they're all coming out."

"They always do in the end."

Elsa-May sighed, and then quoted, *"For nothing is secret, that shall not be made manifest; neither hid, that shall not be known and come abroad."*

CHAPTER 22

Two days later Ettie decided it was time to visit Detective Kelly again, after hearing nothing from him. She'd have to tell him Ebenezer and Levi were brothers. He seemed sure he'd gotten his killer, so it probably wouldn't matter to him.

When they got to the station, they were greeted by a glum-looking Detective Kelly who showed them into his office.

"What's happened with Ebenezer's wife?" Ettie asked.

"Did her blood match your samples?" Elsa-May asked.

He shook his head. "We had to let her go this morning. I still think she's guilty, but these days a jury is reluctant to convict anyone without undisputed forensic evidence." He shook his head. "It shouldn't be like that."

"What about the handwriting?"

The wrinkles in his forehead deepened. "Our experts tell me they don't match. What makes it worse is that it looks like someone was imitating her writing. It wasn't

Elaine's, but it was a good effort." He shook his head. "We can't have strong evidence for each and every case. The system's letting too many go free. I long for the good old days."

"If it wasn't her blood or her handwriting, then why do you still think she did it?" Ettie asked.

"We have other evidence, Mrs. Smith."

Ettie said, "But she cut her hands and went to the hospital on that day. If she'd cut them while she was murdering her estranged husband, surely the blood from her hands would be there. Wouldn't it?"

He ignored her question. "I'm asking people who knew him to volunteer for DNA samples."

"You mean us?" Ettie asked.

He shook his head. "I already have yours on file from another case. Anyway, what can I do for you ladies today?"

"It's what we can do for you. Tell him, Ettie."

When he stared at Ettie, she took a deep breath. "Levi and Ebenezer were brothers." She cringed expecting him to have a bad reaction.

"I know. We found that out when we had a familial DNA match for one of the blood samples we found. Meaning it was from a close family member. It immediately brought to mind the similarities in the two mens' appearances. I confronted Levi Smucker with my suspicions yesterday and he confessed."

Elsa-May gasped and held her head. "Levi killed him! *Ach,* Ettie, it's just like Cain and Abel. One brother killed another."

"No, Mrs. Lutz. Sorry. He confessed to being Ebenezer's brother and that's all. When he found his brother stabbed, he picked up the sharp murder weapon and somehow managed to cut himself with it."

"So, that's two now who cut themselves with the murder weapon? How can that be?"

"The neighbor found Ebenezer, picked up the knife from near the body, and then Levi came across him at that moment, saw the knife in Mr. Simpson's hand and pulled the weapon out of Simpson's hand, thus cutting the neighbor's hand and his own at the same time."

Elsa-May scowled. "That means you have three lots of blood at the scene—besides Ebenezer's?"

"Four. On the second sweep, we found yet another inside the house."

"That's funny, because the nurse came to Helga's on that very day, asked for a glass of water, dropped it and cut her hand on it, also."

Kelly huffed in exasperation. "Drop it with the nurse, Mrs. Smith. She's not guilty and staying focused on her will blind you to other possibilities."

"I'm just saying that—"

"Let's hope we'll be further enlightened when further results come back." He shook his head. "I was so sure it was the wife."

"The poor thing. Where is she now?" Elsa-May asked.

"It's not for me to give out personal information."

"We just want to introduce ourselves and say how sorry we are about Ebenezer. That's all," Ettie said. She reached forward and took hold of a file on his desk that had a small photo clipped to the front. "Is this her?" Ettie asked.

Kelly lunged for it and grabbed it from her. "Mrs. Smith!"

"Let us talk with her, please," Elsa-May said to him.

"I can't give you that information. I'll be back in touch when I have something I can share with you. Meanwhile, keep on with asking questions of anyone and everyone. See what you can turn up."

"We'll show ourselves out." They walked out of the station, and when they were safely up the road, Elsa-May asked, "What did you think of that, Ettie?"

"I don't know. He doesn't give much away, does he? The last time Elaine was staying here, she stayed at Deer Inn. That's what Kelly mentioned. Deer Acres, I mean."

Elsa-May's face brightened up. *"Jah,* so there's a good chance she's staying there now."

"Right. People are generally creatures of habit. Let's go. I know exactly where that place is."

THE SISTERS GOT a taxi to the guest house and walked in through the double doors. They were faced with a reception desk and a middle-aged man behind it. He looked up at them and smiled. "Looking for a room?"

"We're looking for our friend, Elaine Greene."

"That's not her last name, Ettie, remember?"

"Oh, how silly of me. What is her last name?" Ettie looked up at the ceiling trying to remember. "It's a short name." Normally, her memory was good, but she'd had so much on her mind this ... week. "Oh! It's like 'week' but not exactly that. Or Weeks, I'm pretty sure."

He tapped a few keys on his computer. "Yes, I have an Elaine Wicks."

146

"That's her. That's her new name. Thank you. It would have come to me, but these days it can take a long time." She gave a little giggle.

"Where can we find her?" Elsa-May asked.

"Second door on the left."

"Thank you."

They headed down the ornately wallpapered hallway with its thick multi-colored carpet under their feet. Ettie felt like the walls were caving in on her, like she was sinking in quicksand. "I hope she's nice," Ettie said.

"There's one way to find out." Elsa-May moved beyond Ettie and knocked on the mint-colored door.

They heard someone say, "I'm coming."

They waited a couple more minutes before the door opened. The woman was elderly, around the same age Ebenezer would've been. Her hair was covered in a plastic shower cap and she was busy doing up the belt of her pale blue dressing gown.

"I'm sorry. I'm coloring my hair." She looked down at their clothing.

"We knew your husband, Ebenezer," Ettie said. "We hope you don't mind us coming to say hello."

"Oh. Come in." She stepped aside and the two women sat down on a small couch while Elaine sat down on the bed. "They think I did It."

Elsa-May said, "We heard you were arrested and then released. We were just at the police station."

"You were close friends of Ebenezer's?"

"We knew him well enough." Ettie did her best to tell the truth without revealing too much.

Elaine put a hand to her head. "We had a terrible row. It was just the day before he was killed."

"Who do you think killed him?" Elsa-May asked.

"I have no idea. I hope the police find them, though, or they might come after me again."

"Do you know Ebenezer's neighbors?"

"I know the ones who're trying to buy the land from me."

"You own the property Ebenezer's house was on?"

"I do. I own the house, the land, the whole lot. It's been in my family for close on two hundred years. My grandfather once owned all the land around there. Bit by bit, he sold it off. He gave this parcel to me."

"Did you and Ebenezer divorce?" Ettie asked, trying to find out as much as she possibly could.

"No. He was my first love and I was his. I loved him but I just couldn't live with him. I had to leave him. I told him he could move to the land I'd inherited and he moved there and stayed on. I only meant him to live there six months or so, just until he found somewhere else." She shook her head. "He refused to move. Right up to the day he died he was still unwilling to budge."

Then it clicked with Ettie that Elaine was the person trying to force him off the land. "Is that why you fought? Do you want to sell to the neighbors?"

"That's right." She held her head. "I'm making little sense. I've hardly slept and I feel sick to my stomach. I can't wait until I get back home. I've been told to stay around for a few more days."

"Who told you?"

"Detective Kelly." A buzzer sounded. "Ah, I have to rinse the color out of my hair. Do you want to wait? It'll only take me a couple of minutes."

"Go ahead. We'll wait."

"You can make yourself coffee or tea." She pointed to the shelf above the fridge where an electric teakettle sat, along with an assortment of mugs and tea bags and coffee fixings.

"We'll be fine," Ettie said.

Five or ten minutes later, Elaine came out of the bathroom with a towel wrapped around her head. "I like to keep ahead of the grays. I used to be dark blonde, so I stick with that." She sat back on the bed. "I do envy you both. You don't have to worry about your hair because you keep it covered."

"I hadn't ever thought much about it. Mine went gray many years ago. I don't mind it like that."

"Me neither," Elsa-May said. "Getting back to Ebenezer, Ettie and I came here to pay our respects and to offer our condolences."

"Thank you. That's so thoughtful. That's the first touch of humanity I've found since I arrived here in the police car. I think that's what attracted me to Ebenezer at first. It was his goodness and calmness and his quiet personality. Very different from the people I grew up around."

"And you grew up in Walker County?"

"That's right. Close to an Amish community."

"Can I ask something?"

"Go ahead."

Ettie said, "When you married him, did you have plans of joining us?"

"No. I'd made that very clear beforehand. Ebenezer left for me."

"Oh."

"Then when we found we couldn't live together, I left and he went away. That's when I found him living in squalor and I offered him the house on my land here. I knew the house was liveable, and he took up my offer. It seems he re-joined the community when he arrived."

"Did you know his brother?"

"Levi? I knew him. Turns out, he was living less than a mile from my land. *That* I didn't know." She yawned. "I'm sorry, ladies, but is it possible for you to come back tomorrow? I'm in need of sleep."

"Certainly. And we will come back tomorrow, if you don't mind."

"Very well. It was nice to meet people who were close with Ebenezer."

THEY WALKED DOWN THE ROAD. "Did you hear what she said about the neighbors, Ettie?

"*Jah.* Ebenezer was in their way because he wouldn't move."

"But that takes the suspicion off the nurse, doesn't it? And he was in Elaine's way too."

"That's right. "

"I would've liked to learn more, but all the questions left my head. She was very casual. She didn't mind us seeing her dying her hair like she was."

"We knocked on the door when she was in the middle of it. She had no choice."

Elsa-May sighed. "I suppose. But she could have sent us away. We still don't know who killed him. We're no closer. It could've been some stranger that Ebenezer managed to upset."

"Kelly is adamant it wasn't a stranger."

Elsa-May hailed a passing taxi and when it pulled over for them, they slid into the back seat. On the way home, Ettie wondered if there was something staring her in the face that she hadn't yet seen.

CHAPTER 23

THE NEXT MORNING, Ettie sat staring out the window.

"What are you looking at?"

So lost in her thoughts was she that Elsa-May's words jolted her. "The realtor. He's bringing someone to look at the house."

"What's wrong with that?"

Ettie turned to her sister. "It's a waste of time trying to sell a *haus* in weather like this. It makes more sense to me that houses would sell in the spring when the flowers are blooming and the garden is at its best."

"I'll be surprised if it ever sells. It could take years to offload it, but it's not our problem. Come away from the window now, before they see you looking out."

Ettie let go of the curtains and abandoned her chair by the window and sat down on the couch. "There. Are you happy now?"

"*Denke.*" Elsa-May looked at her over the top of her glasses. "Did you see the people?"

"The buyers?"

"Jah."

"I did. They weren't interested. It was a man in his thirties or so. He's not the buyer type."

When they had heard a car door shut, Ettie couldn't resist getting up to look outside again.

"They can't be finished already, surely," Elsa-May said.

"Told you he wouldn't like it. That realtor's wasting his time. I'll have to tell him that." Ettie walked to the door and opened it.

"Wait a minute, Ettie. Are you serious?"

"I am."

Elsa-May abandoned her knitting and followed Ettie out the door. On her way outside, Elsa-May grabbed both their coats.

"Don't bother with that Elsa-May."

"I wouldn't want you to catch your death of a cold. And I'm only just getting over one myself."

"I'm fine." Ettie made her way to the realtor who was getting into his car. "Hold up!"

The realtor looked up at them and smiled widely. After they'd introduced themselves, Ettie said, "You're wasting your time with that house."

"That's what they tell me, but I'm determined to do it. Everything will sell at the right price. That's the first thing I learned when I started as an intern."

"How low will this place go for? I might buy it myself for five dollars."

He laughed. "I don't know the answer to that. I don't have a crystal ball. But I'll keep your offer in mind." After a silent moment, he asked, "Do you know that Amish man who was killed the other day?"

"Jah, he was a member of our community."

"Sad, very sad. Who is the property left to?"

"That's something we don't know. Why does it interest you?"

"He's a realtor, Ettie, he wants the job of selling it obviously."

He grinned revealing his straight white teeth. "That's what I do for a living."

"Don't you have means of finding out who owns what?"

"Normally we can find out but it's in the name of a company."

"A company?"

He pulled a business card out of his top coat pocket. "If you hear of anybody selling please let me know." He grinned widely again.

"Okay we can do that."

"It would be appreciated. I do have someone close to making an offer on this one."

"You do?" Ettie stared at him.

"That's right. You could have new neighbors before you know it. Bye, ladies." He got into his car and drove away.

"Let's get back inside. It's getting quite chilly."

"Did you hear that, Elsa-May? There's someone interested in buying it."

"It could be just talk, Ettie."

CHAPTER 24

ELSA-MAY AND ETTIE went back to Deer Acres the next morning to continue asking Elaine questions. There was no answer to their knocks.

"I wonder if she still asleep," Elsa-May whispered.

"She said she was tired, but it's nearly lunchtime."

The man sitting behind the reception desk had been on the phone when they had walked past him, but now he came walking over to them." She's already checked out."

"When?"

"Late last night. She paid up for four days, and then didn't even stay."

"Oh, dear," Ettie said, wringing her hands.

"She said she'd have something for me today. Do you mind if we check in her room to see if she's left it there?"

He leaned past them and opened the door that wasn't even locked. "There you are. You're lucky the cleaner's running late today." Then he left them there.

"I fear we've made a dreadful mistake, Elsa-May."

"Kelly's going to be very upset and this time not with us."

"Look for clues to where she might've gone, and hurry."

While Elsa-May looked in the bedroom, Ettie checked the bathroom. In the grout between the tiles that made up the floor of the shower, she noticed a black substance. When she leaned closer and put her finger on it, some of it stuck. She smelled it. It had the strong odor of the smell that wafted out from the hair salons when they walked past them. "Elsa-May!"

Elsa-May came hurrying in and saw Ettie bent over. "What is it?"

"Dark brown hair dye. What color did she tell us she died her hair?"

"Dark blonde."

"Exactly, and what color hair did she have in the photo we saw on Kelly's desk?"

"A light color."

"Dark blonde." Ettie stood up and checked the trash in the bathroom; there were no empty cartons, and neither were there any empty hair dye packages in the trash bin in the bedroom. "She's removed the evidence that she dyed her hair at all. This is not good."

"Should we tell Kelly?"

"I guess so." Ettie sank onto the bed. "We should've seen this, Elsa-May. How did we miss it? She had motive, and serious enough cuts on her hand that she sought treatment. Kelly was right."

Elsa-May sat beside her. "Kelly said her blood type didn't match the ones at the scene."

"Maybe the lab mixed up the samples or made an error."

"Call him and tell him what you found."

Ettie stared at the phone on the nightstand, then reached out and picked up the phone's receiver. As soon as he answered, she blurted out, "Detective Kelly, I have something to tell you."

"Mrs. Smith?"

"Yes."

"What is it?"

"You were right about Elaine."

Elsa-May grabbed the phone from Ettie. "You might need to arrest her again. She's dyed her hair dark brown." Then she handed the phone back to Ettie.

"Stop it, Elsa-May."

"Was that Mrs. Lutz?"

"It was."

"Tell her from me that I can't arrest a woman for changing her hair color. If that were so, I'd be arresting my own wife every other month."

Ettie glared at Elsa-May. "It's not just that. We found her staying at Deer Acres and we talked to her last night. She said to come back and talk to her again this morning. Now she's gone."

"How did you know where ... What? She's gone?"

"Not only that, she's died her hair dark brown, like Elsa-May said. She told us she was only covering the grays and going dark blonde, not dark brown."

"Where are you calling from?"

"From the room where she stayed at the Deer Acres Guest House."

"Don't touch anything. Don't move, and I'll be right there." He hung up in her ear.

"He's coming here," Ettie said. "And we're not to touch anything."

"Hmm. Bit late for that."

The man from the front desk stuck his head in the door. "Did she leave what you were looking for?"

"I'm afraid that the police are coming over here right now and they'll want to look through this room."

"The woman was a criminal?"

Ettie shrugged. "Maybe."

"Oh dear. I'll have to check that her payment went through." The man disappeared.

Ettie sighed. "Will Kelly blame us, Elsa-May?"

"Most likely. He wouldn't tell us where she was for a reason. He might say we scared her away."

"Did we?"

"I think she thought everything was closing in on her with all the questions we were asking."

"It's a shame. Killed at the hand of his wife who once loved him."

Elsa-May nodded. "All because he wouldn't get off her land so she could sell it to the neighbors."

As soon as Kelly came with his officers, Ettie and Elsa-May got out of there as fast as they could.

CHAPTER 25

ON MONDAY MORNING, Kelly came to their house. He stood at the door, stony-faced.

"Have you found her?" asked Ettie.

Elsa-May was busy closing Snowy in her bedroom. Snowy was fond of the detective, but that wasn't reciprocated and Snowy made a nuisance of himself every time Kelly was about.

He shook his head. "She disappeared and then she returned one of my messages. She said she left and went home because she was distressed. She's coming back and has agreed to stay put here for a few days."

"That's good of her, but what about her hair color?"

"She insists she hadn't dyed it dark. She said the dye looks dark, but it washes out light."

Elsa-May came back. "What have I missed?"

Kelly stepped into the house and faced Elsa-May squarely. "You're lucky I'm not here with a warrant for your arrest, Mrs. Lutz."

Wide-eyed, she pointed to herself. "Me? Don't you mean Ettie?"

His eyebrows pinched together. "Her blood wasn't found inside Mr. Fuller's house. Yours was!"

"What?" Elsa-May gasped.

"He said—"

"I heard what he said, Ettie." She looked at Kelly. "You don't think I killed him, do you?"

"If I did, I'd be cuffing you right now." He crossed his arms over his chest. "Can you explain how your blood got into Ebenezer's kitchen?"

"Elsa-May, you broke my favorite cup."

Elsa-May scowled at Ettie. "I know. I said I'd replace it. We've got bigger things to think about right now."

"You cut your hand on it. Remember?"

"That's right. I did and I unwrapped the handkerchief I'd wrapped around it when I was in Ebenezer's kitchen." She stared at the detective. "I'd put it on too tight."

He breathed out heavily. "You contaminated the crime scene. A crime scene is paramount to finding the perpetrator. Next time, do what you're told. Keep out and away from crime scenes."

"We didn't—"

Kelly raised his hand to stop Ettie from talking further. "No excuses, just do it. I'm going to need you to come down to the station and make an official statement."

"I can do that. Now?"

"Later today or tomorrow will be fine." He sniffed the air. "Have you been baking?'

"We did earlier today. It's a lemon cake and I've just finished frosting it."

"It smells delicious."

"Do you want to sample some?" Ettie asked.

Kelly grinned. When he was eating—or talking about eating—cake, that was just about the only time they ever saw him smile. "I wouldn't mind, if that's all right."

"Certainly, and would you like coffee with that?"

He chuckled. "Now you're reading my mind."

"Come into the kitchen and we'll fix you something in there. It's warm. We've had the oven on for most of the morning."

Kelly sat at the small round table while Elsa-May cut the cake and Ettie fixed the coffee.

"Have you continued to ask everyone about Ebenezer?" he asked.

"We have. We had a meeting on Sunday and then—"

"That was yesterday," Elsa-May corrected her."

"I know it was yesterday."

"Why didn't you say yesterday?"

"I didn't choose to."

Kelly cleared his throat. "All right. If we can just keep on the topic, that'd be good. You had your meeting yesterday you were saying, Mrs. Smith?"

"That's right and we talked to a lot of people there."

"And what did you find out about Ebenezer?"

"He wasn't a popular man."

"I already knew that," Kelly said. "And the bishop and his wife kept an eye on him too, but probably less frequently than ideal. Did he have any enemies?"

"You don't think the wife did it now?" Elsa-May asked.

Kelly then told Elsa-May the news that Ebenezer's wife had been located. "All I want the both of you to do is question people. Is that too hard?"

"No, it's not. I'm sure we'll find something out soon if

we keep asking." Ettie put a mug of coffee in front of Kelly and sat down, just as Elsa-May also served him a piece of cake.

"This looks delicious. Would you mind if I get the recipe from you for my wife?"

Elsa-May simply glowed at the appreciation of her food. "Certainly. I'll write it up for her before you leave."

"I tell her about your cooking all the time." He took a mouthful of the cake and then his mouth turned down the corners.

"What is it?"

He shook his head and then pulled a large white handkerchief out of his pocket and that's where his mouthful of cake ended up. Then he placed it back in his pocket.

"Was there something wrong?"

He ran his tongue around his mouth. "Taste it and see."

Ettie popped a piece of cake in her mouth and chewed and swallowed it. "Something's wrong for sure."

"What is it, Ettie?" Elsa-May asked.

Ettie jumped up. "The canisters." She picked up the canister on the countertop and opened the lid. "Is this what you used today as flour?"

"Yes, that's the flour."

"No, Elsa-May, this is the salt."

Elsa-May's eyebrows flew up.

"You'll have to wear your glasses while you're baking."

Detective Kelly chuckled and stuck his finger into the frosting and popped it into his mouth. "Good," he said, and scooped up another fingerful.

"Sorry, Detective Kelly. This is the first time, and I hope, the last time I've done anything like this. I'll make another cake and bring it in for you tomorrow. For you and for Mrs. Kelly."

He chuckled. "No need."

"I insist."

"Okay and you can make your statement at the same time. I only hope no one sees the cake as a bribe."

Elsa-May gasped. "Would they?"

He laughed. "No. I was just teasing.

"The coffee I made will be fine."

He picked up the mug and cautiously took a small sip. "Perfect."

Ettie reached up in the cupboard and pulled out a jar of cookies and placed several on his plate.

"Thank you. I hope we can find out something sooner or later. I've got handwriting experts looking at those two notes we found to see if they were written by the same person. There was little else to go on inside the house. It was too clean."

"Cleaner than normal?" Ettie asked.

"Yes, it was and that's what made me suspicious. It was a little too clean and tidy for a single man."

"You think someone made a mess and then came back and cleaned it up?"

Kelly rubbed his lined forehead. "It's possible. That's why I sent the team back the second time for a more thorough going-over in the house, looking for those small details that just don't fit."

"If he wasn't a person to keep to himself so much, he might be alive right now."

"Why do you say that, Mrs. Lutz?"

"More people would've been around his house. There

would've been more people coming and going and someone might've seen something."

"The realtor selling the house next door asked us about Ebenezer's house."

"Those funeral chasers! I've had enough of them."

Ettie raised her eyebrows at Kelly's raised voice. "What do you mean?"

"As soon as someone dies they're looking to profit from it. Whether it's a realtor wanting the listing of the house, or a funeral home wanting the job for the funeral. I don't like it. Antique dealers, they're the worst. They'll knock on the door of the deceased minutes after a death notice goes in the paper."

"Just doing their job, aren't they?" Elsa-May asked.

He shook his head. "There are different ways of approaching things. They could wait until they're contacted." Detective Kelly finished the last of his coffee. Then he pushed out his chair and stood up. "Thank you for the coffee and … the frosting."

"You're welcome and I'll bring a decent cake into the station tomorrow for you and Mrs. Kelly."

"You don't have to do that. Just a recipe or two would keep the wife happy."

"I insist."

"Mrs. Smith, keep the salt away from your sister while she's baking, would you?"

Ettie laughed. "I'll do my best."

Elsa-May's lips turned down at the corners. "I don't think it's funny. What a dreadful mistake to make."

"Anybody could make such a mistake, Elsa-May."

"Would you have?"

Ettie shook her head. "Not me."

Elsa-May groaned. "I don't know how I did that and salt shouldn't ... I should've noticed it had a different texture."

"You were probably upset about Ebenezer. If we find the person who did it perhaps we'll stop another death."

"We're doing all we can to help," Ettie said.

Kelly headed to the door and they followed him. "I'll see you tomorrow perhaps?"

"You will."

Once he was gone, Elsa-May let Snowy out of her bedroom, and both sisters went back into the kitchen.

Elsa-May stood there looking, hands on hips, in disgust at her baking efforts. "Now, what are we going to do with this cake?"

"The only thing we can do is throw it away."

"It seems a waste."

"You eat it then."

Elsa-May sighed. "I suppose you're right."

Ettie picked up the plate of cake. "Why don't you have a little sleep?"

"I can't do that. It's the middle of the day."

"It won't hurt. I won't tell anyone."

"I suppose I could." Elsa-May headed into her bedroom and after Ettie threw the cake in the trash, she sat on the couch pleased and satisfied to have some quiet time to herself. She rarely got time alone during the day, so she closed her eyes and enjoyed the silence. There was no one to reprimand her, no clickety-clack of knitting needles—a constant sound whenever Elsa-May was around, and no one to tell her she could've done things better. Snowy made a giant leap and jumped up beside Ettie and cuddled up next to her.

Ettie closed her eyes and stroked Snowy's long white fur while she pondered who might've killed Ebenezer and why. What made it all the more difficult was the mystery surrounding his coming to the community.

The next thing Ettie knew, someone was shaking her awake.

CHAPTER 26

ETTIE OPENED her heavy eyelids and saw a large dark shape hovering over her. She was startled until she realized it was only her sister.

"I can't sleep," Elsa-May told her.

Ettie blinked in an effort to wake herself a little more. "Did you try?"

"I did."

"You could've let me sleep."

Elsa-May took a couple of steps back and tied the cord of her dressing gown. "I didn't know you were asleep. I thought you might be dead."

"Dead?" That made Ettie bolt to an upright posture on the couch.

"I wasn't sure." Elsa-May spoke calmly as she sat down in her chair.

"Is this what things have come to? Every time I sleep you're going to think I'm dead?"

"I didn't give it too much thought, Ettie. Just that if

you'd died I'd rather know about it now than later on tonight."

Ettie frowned at her sister. "Would it have ruined your dinner plans?"

"*Nee,* but it got me to thinking, where would I live if you'd died?"

Ettie folded her arms, not liking the subject of the conversation. "And what did you decide?"

"I thought I'd live with Ava and Jeremiah. They have the *grossdaddi haus* attached to theirs."

"It sounds like you thought about things for more than a fleeting moment."

Elsa-May picked up her knitting and gone was the last bit of Ettie's peace. "I don't think I'd like to live by myself."

"You'd have Snowy."

"He could come with me to Ava's. I'm sure they wouldn't mind."

Ettie stared at her sister in disbelief. "You've created a whole other life in your head that doesn't include me."

Elsa-May looked over the top of her glasses. "You'd be dead, Ettie."

Ettie opened her mouth not knowing what to say. Anyway, her sister's health wasn't great, so surely, she'd go first and Ettie hadn't planned a life without her. "I'd be dead, would I?"

Elsa-May continued, "In my mind, you were when I was thinking those things."

Snowy jumped down from the couch and scratched at the back door.

"Ah, I locked the dog door." Their conversation was interrupted by Elsa-May unlocking Snowy's door so he could get outside. When Elsa-May headed back to her chair, Ettie wasn't ready to let go of the subject.

"Did you enjoy your new life where I was dead and you were living with Jeremiah and Ava?"

Elsa-May stopped still. "*Nee*. I missed you and the life I have here. Nothing was ever the same again."

Ettie smiled, pleased to hear she'd be missed. "And why?"

Elsa-May didn't sit back down, instead she walked over to Ettie, leaned down and gave her a hug. It was just a quick embrace and a rare moment that they showed their affection.

"I'm not dead just yet," Ettie said.

"Me too," said Elsa-May as she headed back to her chair.

Her words didn't make much sense for someone who was normally so precise.

AT LUNCHTIME THE NEXT DAY, the sisters were delighted when Ava stopped by. They'd only just finished piping the frosting on Kelly's cake and were getting ready to leave. Ava had saved them a taxi fare.

On the way to the station, Ettie was worried. "I hope he's not mad with us again."

"Me too," Elsa-May said.

"What have you found out so far?" asked Ava. "Let's talk our way through it and something might fall into place."

Ettie began, "Okay. I once thought it was the neighbors. I can't remember their names, so I'll call them Jack and Jill."

"And why did you think they did it?" Ava asked.

"I can't say they did it, but he had a bandaged hand. Then there's the nurse—she was the first one to strike me as questionable—who might've been after Ebenezer's money."

"Not likely, Ettie. He never agreed to give her anything," Elsa-May said.

"So she claims. How do you know that? He could've realized the kind of woman she was and then strung her along for the sake of her visits. He might've lied. He wouldn't be the first man who ever lied to a woman."

"That's possible, I suppose, but wouldn't she have made certain of that before she killed him?" Ava asked.

"Well then, it could've been the fruit boy."

"Why?" Ava asked.

"Because ... Ebenezer might've complained about a moldy apple." Elsa-May giggled at her own words.

Ettie shook her head. "Can't you come up with something better?"

Ava laughed and said, "So, the suspects are the neighbors, the nurse, and the fruit boy? Oh, and the wife?"

Slowly, Ettie nodded. "That's about right."

Ava threaded her prayer *kapp* strings through her fingers while she held the reins in one hand. "What about the workers from the farm next door?"

"Jack and Jill's cottonseed farm?" Ettie asked.

"*Jah.*"

"There aren't any. They're all seasonal workers. They don't live there and I don't think Ebenezer would've known any of them. He wasn't the kind of person to make himself known to strangers."

Elsa-May turned around and looked at Ettie. "What about Cain and Abel? It happened once before. What if Levi killed his own *bruder*? He moved and changed his name to get away from him. It must've been a dreadful shock when Ebenezer moved so close to him."

"For what purpose, Elsa-May?"

"Hatred? Loathing, or maybe in anger?"

Ettie groaned. "It's got to be Elaine. She wouldn't have run if she wasn't guilty. It's looking more like her every minute. The only problem with that is, she's come back— and the blood samples didn't match hers. If she was guilty surely she would've kept going. Someone tried to emulate her handwriting with those notes in Ebenezer's *haus*."

"But who and why?" Elsa-May asked.

"When you answer that, you might have your killer," Ava said.

"Then what about the fruit boy and Jack Simpson being friends? That makes no sense."

"I know."

After Ava parked the buggy, Elsa-May took the cake into the station while Ava and Ettie waited in the buggy.

A few minutes later, she was back. "He wasn't there. I left it at the front desk for him."

"Did you make that statement?"

"I asked them, and no one knew I was coming. They asked me to call back later."

"Strange."

"Where to now?" asked Ava. "I've got another hour before I have to get Aaron from *Mamm*."

"Just take us home *denke*, Ava," Ettie said.

SAMANTHA PRICE

~

Ava took them home and before her buggy got to the end of the road, Elsa-May and Ettie saw another buggy approaching.

"Who's that?" Elsa-May asked squinting.

"It's Gabriel."

Elsa-May chuckled. "He always cheers me up. I'll get the teakettle on."

"I'll wait here for him."

Moments later, Gabriel jumped out sporting a wide grin, and hurried over to Ettie. "I can't tell you how happy I am. Oh, where are my manners. How are you on this lovely day, Ettie?"

Ettie glanced up at the gray sky. *Lovely to some,* she thought. "I'm good. Come inside, Elsa-May's putting the teakettle on for a nice cup of *kaffe.*"

"Okay." He took off his hat, wiped his feet and stepped through the door. "I've got the most wonderful news. I asked Selena a question and she agreed."

CHAPTER 27

ETTIE'S MOUTH DROPPED OPEN. That had to mean Selena was joining them and then they were getting married. What else could the question be? "Don't say another word until Elsa-May's here. Elsa-May! Come out here now!"

Elsa-May hurried out of the kitchen tying her work apron around her back. "Hello, Gabriel. What is it, Ettie?"

"Sit down. Gabriel has something to tell us." Ettie held onto Gabriel's arm and guided him to the couch. "Now go on, tell us."

"I have some exciting news. I asked Selena something and she agreed."

Ettie leaned closer. "Is that something you're going to tell us or do we have to guess?"

He threw his head back and laughed. "She's moving into my *haus*." When they looked horrified, he added, "It's not like that. I'm moving out."

"She's moving into your place and you're moving out?"

"That's right, Elsa-May."

"Why would you do that?" Ettie asked.

He faced Ettie. "She had to find somewhere to live in a hurry and she loves my *haus*."

"Where will you go?"

"I just bought the place next door to you."

Elsa-May held her throat. "What?"

"Next door. The empty house. The man sold it to me at a cheap price."

"Do you remember what happened there?" Elsa-May asked.

"*Jah.* Of course. That's why it was cheap, he said."

Ettie couldn't keep the smile from her face. Her prayers had been answered. "That's the best news I've heard in years."

"I'm happy you're pleased, Ettie. And you, Elsa-May?" He looked at Elsa-May.

"I'm in shock. We'd love to have you for a neighbor, Gabriel."

"I might not be there for long because when we're married I'll move back into the other house."

Ettie nodded. "It's good to have a plan, I suppose." After Gabriel talked for a little while about how wonderful Selena was and how beautiful her eyes were, Ettie turned the subject around to Ebenezer.

"You were wrong, Ettie."

Ettie stared at her sister wondering what she was talking about. "About what?"

"You said no one would buy the house in the wintertime and someone did."

Slowly, Ettie nodded. Then she asked Gabriel, "You told us the other day that Ebenezer was sad about something on the last day you saw him."

"That's right he was."

"Have you given much thought to what might have brought on that change in his mood?"

"No, but something else happened while I was there."

"What?" the sisters said in unison.

He swallowed hard. "It might mean nothing, but he didn't have the money to pay for his food delivery. He had it every other time, so I thought it a little weird."

"Food was delivered that day?"

"That's right."

"I paid for it. It wasn't much, but Ebenezer seemed embarrassed that I paid for it."

Elsa-May crossed her legs at her ankles. "Did he normally pay for the food on the day of delivery?"

"*Jah*. He said he hadn't been to the bank this month to get his money."

"Hmm."

"Does that mean something?" he asked.

"I'm not certain what, but maybe it does."

ETTIE WOKE up in the early hours of the morning and couldn't get back to sleep. Then something occurred to her and she hurried into Elsa-May's room.

"Elsa-May, wake up." She shook her sister's shoulder

"What is it?"

"The letters we found. I'm sure they were written in the same handwriting as the notes."

Elsa-May sat up rubbing her eyes. "What letters?"

"The ones that were addressed to the neighbors."

"You're only realizing that now."

"Well, no. I'm not certain."

"Then why wake me?" Elsa-May flopped back onto the bed and turned away from Elsa-May.

Ettie sighed and made herself a cup of hot tea. She knew she wouldn't be able to get back to sleep.

Once Elsa-May was awake, Ettie convinced her they needed to go back to Ebenezer's house and take a look at those letters.

They were walking to call for a taxi when one drove right past them. Elsa-May raised her hand and managed to attract the driver's attention.

IT WAS STILL early in the morning when they walked through the front door of Ebenezer's house.

Ettie went over to where she'd left the letters on the couch. They were still there. She sat down and lifted them onto her lap. Elsa-May sat next to her. "Well, what do you think?" asked Elsa-May. "Is that the same handwriting?"

"I'm certain of it."

"The same person who wanted to meet him at the boundary was writing letters to the neighbors. Read them, Ettie."

Ettie opened the first one and read it quickly. "It's to both of them next door and it's from Elaine. She's plotting with them to get Ebenezer off the land and now we have proof. It was her."

"Is that right?"

"Elsa-May, we're going to have a pre-dinner get together with the people who knew Ebenezer."

"We are?"

"We are. Come along, we've got to write the invitations. I'll have Ava deliver them. I'll even invite Elaine."

CHAPTER 28

TWO EVENINGS LATER, Ettie was pleased when all the people she'd invited had come. Amongst them was Ebenezer's killer. She was certain of it and tonight she was going to coax them into admitting it.

Halfway through the evening, Ettie made her move. She stood up and spoke in a loud voice. "Thank you all for coming. You think you're here for Christmas cake and to bid farewell to our dear friend, Ebenezer."

"Aren't we?" someone in the room called out.

"You're here because you all knew Ebenezer, and his killer is in this room." A hush swept across the room.

"I hope you don't think it was me again," Elaine said.

"Ettie. I hope you're not going to say Levi did it?" Helga said.

"Just listen to her," Elsa-May called out.

Ettie continued, "At first it was obvious. Then too obvious to be true, so all the evidence was swept to one side after excuses were made."

Blythe Simpson said, "Why would you have Patricia

Stuart in your house? A woman with no warmth and no humanity? She's a viper, a vixen, and she was out to get his money."

"Now wait a minute!" Patricia jumped to her feet. "It was probably you or your husband. Gabriel told me you were trying to force Ebenezer out of his house so you could buy his land."

Gabriel stood up. "Now wait a minute. I'm not sure of anything."

Elsa-May stood up. "Everyone keep calm. Sit back down, and let Ettie talk."

One at a time they all sat down. Ettie waited until she was the only one who remained standing.

"This is ridiculous," Pete Ross, the fruit boy, said.

Elsa-May leaned toward him, and shushed him. "Shhh."

"Elaine, did you book into Deer Acres on the day or the days surrounding Ebenezer's death?"

"No and I didn't go to the hospital either and I had no knife marks on my hands like they tried to make out."

"Then what made you choose to stay at Deer Acres when we saw you, if you'd never been there before?"

"The detective accused me of staying there, and I guess that name was in my head when I needed a place to stay after they realized I'd been wrongly arrested. I'm sorry, I know I told you to come back the next day, but I just couldn't stay."

"Don't give it another thought," Elsa-May said.

Ettie looked at Elsa-May clamped her lips and gave a slight shake of her head, telling her to keep quiet. Then she looked at Jack. "Jack, you had cuts on your hands from the murder weapon and so did Levi."

"So what? That doesn't prove anything."

"But lying about it might," she countered.

"Hmmph," he grumbled.

"Patricia, two days before Ebenezer was found dead, you made a large deposit into a bank account. And, I'm guessing you've got more cash hiding somewhere. Ebenezer's money."

Patricia jumped to her feet. "I don't have to listen to this."

"You took Ebenezer's money that he had hidden in his closet. Money that he'd saved over the years and he figured out it had to be you who took it. He threatened to expose you. Then you framed Elaine."

"You're absurd. It's all lies!"

"When you were snooping around his house, you came across some of Ebenezer's wife's identification documents and used them when you booked into the hospital. It wasn't the closest hospital either because you didn't want to bump into someone you knew. Then to further cover your tracks, you booked a room at Deer Acres under Elaine's name. You found the letters from Elaine trying to work with the neighbors to sell them the land if they could get Ebenezer to leave. You copied that handwriting."

Elaine called out. "And she must've forged my writing everywhere she had to sign papers."

"That's right." Ettie nodded, and then turned to Patricia. "What was all that about?"

Jack Simpson yelled out. "She was trying to make us look as though we had something to do with it. My wife never trusted her."

"You're all ridiculous and I'm not going to stay here

another moment and listen to this ridiculousness." She hurried to the door and was met by Detective Kelly who was on the other side.

"Patricia Stuart, you're under arrest for the murder of Ebenezer Fuller. For starters. There's also burglary, elder abuse, forgery and identity theft—and anything else we can dig up."

"I didn't! There's some mistake."

A female officer stepped forward and snapped cuffs on Patricia and, as they took her to the car, Kelly read out her rights.

Everyone was silent, and Elsa-May hurried over to Ettie. "You were right all the time."

"I know. I don't know why no one listened to me. I also didn't get a chance to ask her why she let Gabriel's horses out that day." Ettie looked over at Gabriel to see his mouth turned down at the corners.

"If only I'd gone there after I got the horses back," Gabriel said.

"Can't be helped," Elsa-May said.

"She must've planned to keep you away that day, Gabriel. I'm thinking she was preparing to have a difficult conversation with Ebenezer to make excuses for the missing money. Possibly, she was going to blame you. Maybe when he didn't believe her lies that's when she resorted to murder." Ettie looked over at the neighbors. "You knew him better than you let on, didn't you?"

"We did, but we didn't want to admit it and get involved. That's why we said we didn't know him. We didn't know who killed him, so we saw no harm in zipping our lips."

The wife added, "We moved here to get away from the

crime in the city. The last thing we expected was for our own neighbor to be killed. One good thing that came out of all this was meeting Pete at the funeral. We're having him deliver our groceries now. He's a fine young fellow."

Pete looked at them and smiled.

Ettie looked at Blythe. "Why are you so hostile toward Patricia? How did you know she was being harmful to Ebenezer?"

"Ebenezer repeated some of the things she'd said about us and we knew she was poisoning his mind against us."

"What was she saying?" asked Elsa-May.

"We look like people not to be trusted and then she said she was sure my husband was the same man who staggered through the town drunk every Friday night. She told him he was better off to keep to himself."

Gabriel nodded. "I know she didn't like me being there at his house either. She didn't say anything, but I could feel the hostility."

Ettie leaned against a wall glad everything was over. She was a little annoyed with Kelly for having constantly insisted Patricia had nothing to do with it. Hopefully, next time he saw them he would admit he overlooked some things that were obvious.

CHAPTER 29

THE NEXT EVENING, Detective Kelly came to visit the sisters and they were anxious to hear if Patricia had confessed. He sat down in their living room.

"The investigation's over. She eventually confessed when she found out we had evidence."

Ettie heaved a sigh of relief.

"Ebenezer confronted her when he realized she'd taken his money. It was more than fifty thousand dollars that he'd managed to save over the years. He grabbed her arm and wouldn't let her go. To get away from him, she grabbed a knife and stabbed him. Then she dragged him out into the woods behind the barn. I think she was intending to move the body away so it would look like he'd simply disappeared, but he was found before she could do it."

"That's why the house was so clean, Elsa-May. Remember how Helga said it was so neat and even had fresh flowers?"

"I do."

Ettie frowned. "One thing I can't understand is the blood samples. Didn't you ask her for a DNA sample in the first instance?"

"We did, but the DNA sample she gave us and the one we took now that she's in jail, don't match. It seems she switched samples somehow right after the first test was performed."

"So she's the missing blood match?"

"That's right, and she booked herself into the hospital pretending to be Ebenezer's wife. The intake nurse identified her from a photo."

"Just like you thought, Ettie."

"I know." Ettie stared at Kelly. "I told you she was always wearing gloves. That was to cover up her wounds. If you'd listened to me at the beginning you would've saved yourself time."

Kelly pressed his lips together. "Don't think you're so smart, Ettie."

Ettie's mouth fell open. "I don't."

"Ettie was right though," Elsa-May said in her sister's defence.

"You thought it was her to start with, and then you were convinced it was Elaine." He smiled smugly.

That made Ettie upset. She had only dismissed Patricia because of the false evidence and surely that was Kelly's fault. "Detective Kelly, let's play a little game."

"A game?"

"Yes. Would you rather have cake or cookies?"

He frowned and then said, "Cake. Depending on what kind it is and what kind of cookies."

Ettie shook her head. "That's not how this works. You have to pick one or the other."

"Well, then … cake."

"Would you rather it rain on one of your days off or be sunny?"

"I hardly ever have a day off as you know."

"One or the other," Ettie repeated.

He eyed them both carefully. "What's going on here?"

"Would you rather the rest of your hair fall out or lose all your teeth?" Elsa-May asked.

He slowly rose to his feet. "I just remembered I've got somewhere I need to be." He hurried to the door and opened it, took a look over his shoulder at them, and closed the door behind him.

Ettie giggled. She held her stomach and laughed so hard she slid off the couch and thought she'd be ill. Elsa-May held her belly, laughing too, and laughed even harder when she saw Ettie on the floor. Ettie wiped her eyes and picked herself up off the rug. "I haven't laughed so much for a long time."

"Did you see his face?"

"I did." Ettie giggled again and had to wipe a tear from her eye.

"It's amazing the lessons the young can teach us. That game has some uses after all. Now, on a different subject I have something I was going to give you on Christmas, but it's close enough."

Ettie sat up straight. "A gift?"

"Kind of." Elsa-May went into her room and came back with a cardboard box and stretched out her hands to Ettie. "I haven't had time to wrap it."

Ettie looked at the box, and Elsa-May placed it into her hands. "What could it be?"

"Open it and see."

When Ettie opened it, she saw the very thing for which she was hoping. She pulled out a white china teacup with small pink rosebuds. "It's exactly the same." Then she pulled out the saucer and set them both on the table in front of her. *"Denke,* Elsa-May. This is truly thoughtful."

"I'll make you a cup of hot tea right now."

"That would be *wunderbaar.*" Ettie sat looking at the flames flickering in the stone surrounds of the fireplace. What more could she want right at this moment? Hot tea in a favorite cup, made by someone other than her, sitting warm by the fire, and Snowy cuddled up asleep in the corner.

Elsa-May placed the tea down in front of Ettie. "I'd say the cup and saucer could be your Christmas present, but I know you'll want something to open on our gift-giving day."

Ettie giggled, reaching for the tea. Her sister knew her far too well.

Thank you for reading Amish Winter Murder Mystery.

Book 20
Amish Scarecrow Murders

While Ettie Smith is grappling with a pain in her back, a far more sinister agony sweeps through her peaceful community. Two lives, connected to their serene world, have been reaped in the most horrifying manner, sowing seeds of fear in everyone's heart.

As the mystery grows as tall as a cornfield, one haunting detail stands out: each victim's front yard is adorned with a scarecrow, a silent, eerie sentinel. Is the community now a field in a harrowing harvest of death, reminiscent of the unsolved scarecrow murders of the sixties? Or is there a copycat, a straw man who finds inspiration in past terrors?

In the face of danger, just how close can Ettie tread to the scarecrow slayer without finding herself under his ominous gaze? Is she about to make a blunder that could cost more than a bountiful harvest?

Prepare for a story that's more chilling than a midnight encounter with a field of scarecrows. Grab your copy now, and join Ettie in unearthing a mystery that will keep you guessing until the last stalk of corn is counted.

ABOUT SAMANTHA PRICE

Samantha Price is a USA Today bestselling and Kindle All Stars author of Amish romance books and cozy mysteries. She was raised Brethren and has a deep affinity for the Amish way of life, which she has explored extensively with over a decade of research.

She is mother to two pampered rescue cats, and a very spoiled staffy with separation issues.

www.SamanthaPriceAuthor.com

ETTIE SMITH AMISH MYSTERIES

ALL SAMANTHA PRICE BOOK SERIES

Amish Maids Trilogy

Amish Love Blooms

Amish Misfits

The Amish Bonnet Sisters

Amish Women of Pleasant Valley

Ettie Smith Amish Mysteries

Amish Secret Widows' Society

Expectant Amish Widows

Seven Amish Bachelors

Amish Foster Girls